Ambrose Briece

In the midst of life

Tales of soldiers and civilians

Ambrose Briece

In the midst of life
Tales of soldiers and civilians

ISBN/EAN: 9783337118280

Printed in Europe, USA, Canada, Australia, Japan

Cover: Foto ©Andreas Hilbeck / pixelio.de

More available books at **www.hansebooks.com**

IN THE MIDST OF LIFE

TALES OF SOLDIERS AND CIVILIANS

BY

AMBROSE BIERCE

———

G. P. PUTNAM'S SONS
NEW YORK AND LONDON
The Knickerbocker Press
1898

The Tales by Title

Soldiers

I

A Horseman in the Sky

ONE sunny afternoon in the autumn of
the year 1861, a soldier lay in a clump
of laurel by the side of a road in Western
Virginia.   He lay at full length, upon his
stomach, his feet resting upon the toes, his
head upon the left forearm.   His extended
right hand loosely grasped his rifle.   But
for the somewhat methodical disposition of
his limbs and a slight rhythmic movement
of the cartridge-box at the back of his belt,
he might have been thought to be dead.
He was asleep at his post of duty.   But if
detected he would be dead shortly afterward,
that being the just and legal penalty of his
crime.

The clump of laurel in which the criminal
lay was in the angle of a road which, after
ascending, southward, a steep acclivity to

that point, turned sharply to the west, running along the summit for perhaps one hundred yards. There it turned southward
again and went zigzagging downward
through the forest. At the salient of that
second angle was a large flat rock, jutting
out northward, overlooking the deep valley
from which the road ascended. The rock
capped a high cliff; a stone dropped from
its outer edge would have fallen sheer downward one thousand feet to the tops of the
pines. The angle where the soldier lay was
on another spur of the same cliff. Had he
been awake, he would have commanded a
view, not only of the short arm of the road
and the jutting rock, but of the entire profile of the cliff below it. It might well have
made him giddy to look.

The country was wooded everywhere except at the bottom of the valley to the northward, where there was a small natural
meadow, through which flowed a stream
scarcely visible from the valley's rim. This
open ground looked hardly larger than an
ordinary door-yard, but was really several
acres in extent. Its green was more vivid
than that of the inclosing forest. Away be-

yond it rose a line of giant cliffs similar to those upon which we are supposed to stand in our survey of the savage scene, and through which the road had somehow made its climb to the summit. The configuration of the valley, indeed, was such that from this point of observation it seemed entirely shut in, and one could not but have wondered how the road which found a way out of it had found a way into it, and whence came and whither went the waters of the stream that parted the meadow two thousand feet below.

No country is so wild and difficult but men will make it a theatre of war ; concealed in the forest at the bottom of that military rat-trap, in which half a hundred men in possession of the exits might have starved an army to submission, lay five regiments of Federal infantry. They had marched all the previous day and night and were resting. At nightfall they would take to the road again, climb to the place where their unfaithful sentinel now slept, and, descending the other slope of the ridge, fall upon a camp of the enemy at about midnight. Their hope was to surprise it, for the road led to the rear of it. In case of failure, their position would be perilous in the extreme ; and fail they surely would, should accident or vigilance apprise the enemy of the movement.

The sleeping sentinel in the clump of laurel was a young Virginian named Carter Druse. He was the son of wealthy parents, an only child, and had known such ease and cultivation and high living as wealth and taste were able to command in the mountain country of Western Virginia. His home was but a few miles from where he now lay. One morning he had risen from the breakfast-table and said, quietly but gravely : "Father, a Union regiment has arrived at Grafton. I am going to join it."

The father lifted his leonine head, looked at the son a moment in silence, and replied : "Well, go, sir, and, whatever may occur, do what you conceive to be your duty. Virginia, to which you are a traitor, must get on without you. Should we both live to the end of the war, we will speak further of the matter. Your mother, as the physician has informed you, is in a most critical condition ; at the best she cannot be with us longer than a few weeks, but that time is precious. It would be better not to disturb her.''

So Carter Druse, bowing reverently to his father, who returned the salute with a stately courtesy which masked a breaking heart, left the home of his childhood to go soldiering. By conscience and courage, by deeds of devotion and daring, he soon commended himself to his fellows and his officers ; and it was to these qualities and to some knowledge of the country that he owed his selection for his present perilous duty at the extreme outpost. Nevertheless, fatigue had been stronger than resolution, and he had fallen asleep. What good or bad angel came in a dream to rouse him from his state of crime, who shall say ? Without a movement, without a sound, in the profound silence and the languor of the late afternoon, some invisible messenger of fate touched with unsealing finger the eyes of his consciousness—whispered into the ear of his spirit the mysterious awakening word which no human lips ever have spoken, no human memory ever has recalled. He quietly raised his forehead from his arm and looked between the masking stems of the laurels, instinctively closing his right hand about the stock of his rifle.

His first feeling was a keen artistic delight. On a colossal pedestal, the cliff,—motionless at the extreme edge of the capping rock and sharply outlined against the sky,—was an equestrian statue of impressive dignity. The figure of the man sat the figure of the horse, straight and soldierly, but with the repose of a Grecian god carved in the marble which limits the suggestion of activity. The gray costume harmonized with its aërial background; the metal of accoutrement and caparison was softened and subdued by the shadow; the animal's skin had no points of high light. A carbine, strikingly foreshortened, lay across the pommel of the saddle, kept in place by the right hand grasping it at the "grip"; the left hand, holding the bridle rein, was invisible. In silhouette against the sky, the profile of the horse was cut with the sharpness of a cameo; it looked across the heights of air to the confronting cliffs beyond. The face of the rider, turned slightly away, showed only an outline of temple and beard;

he was looking downward to the bottom of
the valley. Magnified by its lift against the
sky and by the soldier's testifying sense of
the formidableness of a near enemy, the
group appeared of heroic, almost colossal,
size.

For an instant Druse had a strange, half-
defined feeling that he had slept to the end
of the war and was looking upon a noble
work of art reared upon that commanding
eminence to commemorate the deeds of an
heroic past of which he had been an inglorious part. The feeling was dispelled by a
slight movement of the group : the horse,
without moving its feet, had drawn its body
slightly backward from the verge ; the man
remained immobile as before. Broad awake
and keenly alive to the significance of the
situation, Druse now brought the butt of his
rifle against his cheek by cautiously pushing
the barrel forward through the bushes,
cocked the piece, and, glancing through the
sights, covered a vital spot of the horseman's
breast. A touch upon the trigger and all
would have been well with Carter Druse.
At that instant the horseman turned his
head and looked in the direction of his con-

cealed foeman—seemed to look into his very
face, into his eyes, into his brave, compas-
sionate heart.

Is it, then, so terrible to kill an enemy in
war—an enemy who has surprised a secret
vital to the safety of one's self and comrades
—an enemy more formidable for his knowledge than all his army for its numbers?
Carter Druse grew pale ; he shook in every
limb, turned faint, and saw the statuesque
group before him as black figures, rising,
falling, moving unsteadily in arcs of circles
in a fiery sky.   His hand fell away from his
weapon, his head slowly dropped until his
face rested on the leaves in which he lay.
This courageous gentleman and hardy soldier was near swooning from intensity of
emotion.

It was not for long ; in another moment
his face was raised from earth, his hands resumed their places on the rifle, his forefinger
sought the trigger ; mind, heart, and eyes
were clear, conscience and reason sound.
He could not hope to capture that enemy ;
to alarm him would but send him dashing
to his camp with his fatal news.   The duty
of the soldier was plain : the man must be

shot dead from ambush—without warning, without a moment's spiritual preparation, with never so much as an unspoken prayer, he must be sent to his account. But no— there is a hope ; he may have discovered nothing—perhaps he is but admiring the sublimity of the landscape. If permitted, he may turn and ride carelessly away in the direction whence he came. Surely it will be possible to judge at the instant of his withdrawing whether he knows. It may well be that his fixity of attention—Druse turned his head and looked through the deeps of air downward as from the surface to the bottom of a translucent sea. He saw creeping across the green meadow a sinuous line of figures of men and horses—some foolish commander was permitting the sol- diers of his escort to water their beasts in the open, in plain view from a hundred summits !

Druse withdrew his eyes from the valley and fixed them again upon the group of man and horse in the sky, and again it was through the sights of his rifle. But this time his aim was at the horse. In his mem- ory, as if they were a divine mandate, rang

the words of his father at their parting :
" Whatever may occur, do what you conceive to be your duty."   He was calm now.
His teeth were firmly but not rigidly closed ;
his nerves were as tranquil as a sleeping
babe's—not a tremor affected any muscle of
his body ; his breathing, until suspended in
the act of taking aim, was regular and slow.
Duty had conquered ; the spirit had said to
the body : " Peace, be still."   He fired.

An officer of the Federal force, who, in a
spirit of adventure or in quest of knowledge,
had left the hidden *bivouac* in the valley,
and, with aimless feet, had made his way to
the lower edge of a small open space near
the foot of the cliff, was considering what
he had to gain by pushing his exploration
further.   At a distance of a quarter-mile
before him, but apparently at a stone's
throw, rose from its fringe of pines the
gigantic face of rock, towering to so great a
height above him that it made him giddy to
look up to where its edge cut a sharp, rugged
line against the sky.   At some distance
away to his right it presented a clean, vertical profile against a background of blue sky
to a point half the way down, and of dis-

tant hills hardly less blue thence to the tops
of the trees at its base.   Lifting his eyes to
the dizzy altitude of its summit, the officer
saw an astonishing sight—a man on horse-
back riding down into the valley through
the air !

Straight upright sat the rider, in military
fashion, with a firm seat in the saddle, a
strong clutch upon the rein to hold his
charger from too impetuous a plunge. From
his bare head his long hair streamed upward, waving like a plume. His hands
were concealed in the cloud of the horse's
lifted mane.   The animal's body was as
level as if every hoof-stroke encountered the
resistant earth.   Its motions were those of a
wild gallop, but even as the officer looked
they ceased, with all the legs thrown sharply
forward as in the act of alighting from a
leap.   But this was a flight !

Filled with amazement and terror by this
apparition of a horseman in the sky—half
believing himself the chosen scribe of some
new Apocalypse, the officer was overcome
by the intensity of his emotions ; his legs
failed him and he fell.   Almost at the same
instant he heard a crashing sound in the

trees—a sound that died without an echo —and all was still.

The officer rose to his feet, trembling. The familiar sensation of an abraded shin recalled his dazed faculties. Pulling himself together, he ran rapidly obliquely away from the cliff to a point distant from its foot; thereabout he expected to find his man; and thereabout he naturally failed. In the fleeting instant of his vision his imagination had been so wrought upon by the apparent grace and ease and intention of the marvellous performance that it did not occur to him that the line of march of aërial cavalry is directly downward, and that he could find the objects of his search at the very foot of the cliff. A half-hour later he returned to camp.

This officer was a wise man; he knew better than to tell an incredible truth. He said nothing of what he had seen. But when the commander asked him if in his scout he had learned anything of advantage to the expedition, he answered:

"Yes, sir; there is no road leading down into this valley from the southward."

The commander, knowing better, smiled.

After firing his shot, Private Carter Druse
reloaded his rifle and resumed his watch.
Ten minutes had hardly passed when a Federal sergeant crept cautiously to him on
hands and knees. Druse neither turned his
head nor looked at him, but lay without
motion or sign of recognition.

"Did you fire?" the sergeant whispered.

"Yes."

"At what?"

"A horse. It was standing on yonder
rock—pretty far out. You see it is no longer
there. It went over the cliff."

The man's face was white, but he showed
no other sign of emotion. Having answered,
he turned away his eyes and said no more.
The sergeant did not understand.

"See here, Druse," he said, after a moment's silence, "it's no use making a mystery. I order you to report. Was there
anybody on the horse?"

"Yes."

"Well?"

"My father."

The sergeant rose to his feet and walked
away. "Good God!" he said.

An Occurrence at Owl Creek Bridge

I

A MAN stood upon a railroad bridge in Northern Alabama, looking down into the swift waters twenty feet below. The man's hands were behind his back, the wrists bound with a cord. A rope loosely encircled his neck. It was attached to a stout cross-timber above his head, and the slack fell to the level of his knees. Some loose boards laid upon the sleepers supporting the metals of the railway supplied a footing for him, and his executioners—two private soldiers of the Federal army, directed by a sergeant, who in civil life may have been a deputy sheriff. At a short remove upon the same temporary platform was an officer in the uniform of his rank, armed. He was a captain. A sentinel at each end of the bridge stood with his rifle in the position known as "support," that is to say, vertical in front of the left shoulder, the hammer resting on the forearm thrown straight across the chest—a formal and unnatural position, enforcing an erect carriage of the body. It did not appear to be the duty of these two men to know what was occurring at the centre of the bridge ; they merely blockaded the two ends of the foot plank which traversed it.

Beyond one of the sentinels, nobody was in sight ; the railroad ran straight away into a forest for a hundred yards, then, curving, was lost to view. Doubtless there was an outpost farther along. The other bank of the stream was open ground—a gentle acclivity crowned with a stockade of vertical tree trunks, loopholed for rifles, with a single embrasure through which protruded the muzzle of a brass cannon commanding the bridge. Midway of the slope between bridge and fort were the spectators—a single company of infantry in line, at "parade rest," the butts of the rifles on the ground, the barrels inclining slightly backward against the right shoulder, the hands crossed upon the stock. A lieutenant stood at the right of the line, the point of his sword upon the ground, his left hand resting upon his right. Excepting the group of four at the centre of the bridge, not a man moved. The company faced the bridge, staring stonily, motionless. The sentinels, facing the banks of the stream, might have been statues to adorn the bridge. The captain stood with folded arms, silent, observing the work of his subordinates, but making no sign. Death is a dignitary who, when he comes announced, is to be received with formal manifestations of respect, even by those most familiar with him. In the code of military etiquette, silence and fixity are forms of deference.

The man who was engaged in being hanged was apparently about thirty-five years of age. He was a civilian, if one might judge from his habit, which was that of a planter. His features were good—a straight nose, firm mouth, broad forehead, from which his long, dark hair was combed straight back, falling behind his ears to the collar of his well-fitting frock-coat. He wore a mustache and pointed beard, but no whiskers ; his eyes were large and dark gray and had a kindly expression which one would hardly have expected in one whose neck was in the hemp. Evidently this was no vulgar assassin. The liberal military code makes provision for hanging many kinds of persons, and gentlemen are not excluded.

The preparations being complete, the two private soldiers stepped aside and each drew away the plank upon which he had been standing. The sergeant turned to the captain, saluted, and placed himself immediately behind that officer, who in turn moved apart one pace. These movements left the condemned man and the sergeant standing on the two ends of the same plank, which spanned three of the cross-ties of the bridge. The end upon which the civilian stood almost, but not quite, reached a fourth. This plank had been held in place by the weight of the captain ; it was now held by that of the sergeant. At a signal from the former, the latter would step aside, the plank would tilt and the condemned man go down

between two ties. The arrangement commended itself to his judgment as simple and
effective. His face had not been covered
nor his eyes bandaged. He looked a moment at his "unsteadfast footing," then let
his gaze wander to the swirling water of
the stream racing madly beneath his feet.
A piece of dancing driftwood caught his
attention and his eyes followed it down the
current. How slowly it appeared to move!
What a sluggish stream!

He closed his eyes in order to fix his last
thoughts upon his wife and children. The
water, touched to gold by the early sun, the
brooding mists under the banks at some distance down the stream, the fort, the soldiers,
the piece of drift—all had distracted him.
And now he became conscious of a new disturbance. Striking through the thought
of his dear ones was a sound which he could
neither ignore nor understand, a sharp, distinct, metallic percussion like the stroke of
a blacksmith's hammer upon the anvil ; it
had the same ringing quality. He wondered what it was, and whether immeasur-
ably distant or near by—it seemed both.
Its recurrence was regular, but as slow as

the tolling of a death knell. He awaited each stroke with impatience and—he knew not why—apprehension. The intervals of silence grew progressively longer ; the delays became maddening. With their greater infrequency the sounds increased in strength and sharpness. They hurt his ear like the thrust of a knife ; he feared he should shriek. What he heard was the ticking of his watch.

He unclosed his eyes and saw again the water below him. "If I could free my hands," he thought, "I might throw off the noose and spring into the stream. By diving I could evade the bullets, and, swimming vigorously, reach the bank, take to the woods, and get away home. My home, thank God, is as yet outside their lines ; my wife and little ones are still beyond the invader's farthest advance."

As these thoughts, which have here to be set down in words, were flashed into the doomed man's brain rather than evolved from it, the captain nodded to the sergeant. The sergeant stepped aside.

II

Peyton Farquhar was a well-to-do planter, of an old and highly respected Alabama family. Being a slave owner, and, like other slave owners, a politician, he was naturally an original secessionist and ardently devoted to the Southern cause. Circumstances of an imperious nature, which it is unnecessary to relate here, had prevented him from taking service with the gallant army which had fought the disastrous campaigns ending with the fall of Corinth, and he chafed under the inglorious restraint, longing for the release of his energies, the larger life of the soldier, the opportunity for distinction. That opportunity, he felt, would come, as it comes to all in war time. Meanwhile he did what he could. No service was too humble for him to perform in aid of the South, no adventure too perilous for him to undertake if consistent with the character of a civilian who was at heart a soldier, and who in good faith and without too much qualification assented to at least a part of the frankly villainous dictum that all is fair in love and war.

One evening while Farquhar and his wife were sitting on a rustic bench near the entrance to his grounds, a gray-clad soldier rode up to the gate and asked for a drink of water. Mrs. Farquhar was only too happy to serve him with her own white hands. While she was gone to fetch the water her husband approached the dusty horseman and inquired eagerly for news from the front.

"The Yanks are repairing the railroads," said the man, "and are getting ready for another advance. They have reached the Owl Creek bridge, put it in order, and built a stockade on the north bank. The commandant has issued an order, which is posted everywhere, declaring that any civilian caught interfering with the railroad, its bridges, tunnels, or trains, will be summarily hanged. I saw the order."

"How far is it to the Owl Creek bridge?" Farquhar asked.

"About thirty miles."

"Is there no force on this side the creek?"

"Only a picket post half a mile out, on the railroad, and a single sentinel at this end of the bridge."

"Suppose a man—a civilian and student of hanging—should elude the picket post and perhaps get the better of the sentinel," said Farquhar, smiling, "what could he accomplish?"

The soldier reflected. "I was there a month ago," he replied. "I observed that the flood of last winter had lodged a great quantity of driftwood against the wooden pier at this end of the bridge. It is now dry and would burn like tow."

The lady had now brought the water, which the soldier drank. He thanked her ceremoniously, bowed to her husband, and rode away. An hour later, after nightfall, he repassed the plantation, going northward in the direction from which he had come. He was a Federal scout.

III

As Peyton Farquhar fell straight downward through the bridge, he lost consciousness and was as one already dead. From this state he was awakened—ages later, it seemed to him—by the pain of a sharp pressure upon his throat, followed by a sense of suffocation. Keen, poignant agonies seemed to shoot from his neck downward through every fibre of his body and limbs. These pains appeared to flash along well-defined lines of ramification and to beat with an inconceivably rapid periodicity. They seemed like streams of pulsating fire heating him to an intolerable temperature. As to his head, he was conscious of nothing but a feeling of fulness—of congestion. These sensations were unaccompanied by thought. The intellectual part of his nature was already effaced; he had power only to feel, and feeling was torment. He was conscious of motion. Encompassed in a luminous cloud, of which he was now merely the fiery heart, without material substance, he swung through unthinkable arcs of oscillation, like a vast pendulum. Then all at once, with terrible suddenness, the light about him shot upward with the noise of a loud plash; a frightful roaring was in his ears, and all was cold and dark. The power of thought was restored; he knew that the rope had broken and he had fallen into the stream. There was no additional strangulation; the noose about his neck was already suffocating him and kept the water from his lungs. To die of hanging at the bottom of a river!—the idea seemed to him ludicrous. He opened his eyes in the darkness and saw above him a gleam of light, but how distant, how inaccessible! He was still sinking, for the light became fainter and fainter until it was a mere glimmer. Then it began to grow and brighten, and he knew that he was rising toward the surface—knew it with reluctance, for he was now very comfortable. "To be hanged and drowned," he thought, "that is not so bad; but I do not wish to be shot. No; I will not be shot; that is not fair."

He was not conscious of an effort, but a sharp pain in his wrists apprised him that he was trying to free his hands. He gave the struggle his attention, as an idler might observe the feat of a juggler, without interest in the outcome. What splendid effort!—what magnificent, what superhuman strength! Ah, that was a fine endeavor! Bravo! The cord fell away; his arms parted and floated upward, the hands dimly seen on each side in the growing light. He watched them with a new interest as first one and then the

other pounced upon the noose at his neck.
They tore it away and thrust it fiercely
aside, its undulations resembling those of a
water-snake. " Put it back, put it back ! "
He thought he shouted these words to his
hands, for the undoing of the noose had
been succeeded by the direst pang which he
had yet experienced. His neck ached horribly ; his brain was on fire ; his heart,
which had been fluttering faintly, gave a
great leap, trying to force itself out at his
mouth. His whole body was racked and
wrenched with an insupportable anguish !
But his disobedient hands gave no heed to
the command. They beat the water vigorously with quick, downward strokes, forcing
him to the surface. He felt his head emerge ;
his eyes were blinded by the sunlight ; his
chest expanded convulsively, and with a
supreme and crowning agony his lungs en-
gulfed a great draught of air, which instantly
he expelled in a shriek !

He was now in full possession of his physical senses. They were, indeed, preternatu-
rally keen and alert. Something in the
awful disturbance of his organic system
had so exalted and refined them that they

made record of things never before perceived. He felt the ripples upon his face and heard their separate sounds as they struck. He looked at the forest on the bank of the stream, saw the individual trees, the leaves and the veining of each leaf—saw the very insects upon them, the locusts, the brilliant-bodied flies, the gray spiders stretching their webs from twig to twig. He noted the prismatic colors in all the dewdrops upon a million blades of grass. The humming of the gnats that danced above the eddies of the stream, the beating of the dragon-flies' wings, the strokes of the water-spiders' legs, like oars which had lifted their boat—all these made audible music. A fish slid along beneath his eyes and he heard the rush of its body parting the water.

He had come to the surface facing down the stream ; in a moment the visible world seemed to wheel slowly round, himself the pivotal point, and he saw the bridge, the fort, the soldiers upon the bridge, the captain, the sergeant, the two privates, his executioners. They were in silhouette. against the blue sky. They shouted and gesticulated, pointing at him ; the captain had

drawn his pistol, but did not fire ; the others
were unarmed.   Their movements were grotesque and horrible, their forms gigantic.

Suddenly he heard a sharp report and
something struck the water smartly within
a few inches of his head, spattering his face
with spray.   He heard a second report, and
saw one of the sentinels with his rifle at his
shoulder, a light cloud of blue smoke rising from the muzzle.   The man in the water
saw the eye of the man on the bridge gazing
into his own through the sights of the rifle.
He observed that it was a gray eye, and remembered having read that gray eyes were
keenest and that all famous marksmen
had them.   Nevertheless, this one had
missed.

A counter swirl had caught Farquhar and
turned him half round ; he was again looking into the forest on the bank opposite the
fort.   The sound of a clear, high voice in a
monotonous singsong now rang out behind
him and came across the water with a distinctness that pierced and subdued all other
sounds, even the beating of the ripples in his
ears. Although no soldier, he had frequented
camps enough to know the dread significance

of that deliberate, drawling, aspirated chant ; the lieutenant on shore was taking a part in the morning's work.   How coldly and pitilessly—with what an even, calm intonation, presaging and enforcing tranquillity in the men—with what accurately measured intervals fell those cruel words :

" Attention, company ! . . . Shoulder arms ! . . . Ready ! . . . Aim ! . . . Fire ! "

Farquhar dived—dived as deeply as he could.   The water roared in his ears like the voice of Niagara, yet he heard the dulled thunder of the volley, and, rising again toward the surface, met shining bits of metal, singularly flattened, oscillating slowly downward.   Some of them touched him on the face and hands, then fell away, continuing their descent.   One lodged between his collar and neck ; it was uncomfortably warm, and he snatched it out.

As he rose to the surface, gasping for breath, he saw that he had been a long time under water ; he was perceptibly farther down stream—nearer to safety.   The soldiers had almost finished reloading ; the metal ramrods flashed all at once in the sunshine as they were drawn from the barrels, turned in the air, and thrust into their sockets.   The two sentinels fired again, independently and ineffectually.

The hunted man saw all this over his shoulder ; he was now swimming vigorously with the current.   His brain was as ener-getic as his arms and legs ; he thought with the rapidity of lightning.

" The officer," he reasoned, " will not make that martinet's error a second time. It is as easy to dodge a volley as a single shot.   He has probably already given the command to fire at will.   God help me, I cannot dodge them all ! "

An appalling plash within two yards of him, followed by a loud, rushing sound, *diminuendo*, which seemed to travel back through the air to the fort and died in an explosion which stirred the very river to its deeps ! A rising sheet of water, which curved over him, fell down upon him, blinded him, strangled him !   The cannon had taken a hand in the game.   As he shook his head free from the commotion of the smitten water, he heard the deflected shot humming through the air ahead, and in an instant it

was cracking and smashing the branches in
the forest beyond.

"They will not do that again," he
thought; "the next time they will use a
charge of grape. I must keep my eye upon
the gun; the smoke will apprise me—the report arrives too late; it lags behind the missile. That is a good gun."

Suddenly he felt himself whirled round
and round—spinning like a top. The water,
the banks, the forest, the now distant bridge.
fort and men—all were commingled and
blurred. Objects were represented by their
colors only; circular horizontal streaks of
color—that was all he saw. He had been
caught in a vortex and was being whirled on
with a velocity of advance and gyration
which made him giddy and sick. In a few
moments he was flung upon the gravel at
the foot of the left bank of the stream—the
southern bank—and behind a projecting
point which concealed him from his enemies.
The sudden arrest of his motion, the abrasion
of one of his hands on the gravel, restored
him, and he wept with delight. He dug his
fingers into the sand, threw it over himself
in handfuls and audibly blessed it. It looked

like diamonds, rubies, emeralds ; he could think of nothing beautiful which it did not resemble. The trees upon the bank were giant garden plants ; he noted a definite order in their arrangement, inhaled the fragrance of their blooms. A strange, roseate light shone through the spaces among their trunks, and the wind made in their branches the music of æolian harps. He had no wish to perfect his escape, was content to remain in that enchanting spot until retaken.

A whiz and rattle of grapeshot among the branches high above his head roused him from his dream. The baffled cannoneer had fired him a random farewell. He sprang to his feet, rushed up the sloping bank, and plunged into the forest.

All that day he travelled, laying his course by the rounding sun. The forest seemed interminable ; nowhere did he discover a break in it, not even a woodman's road. He had not known that he lived in so wild a region. There was something uncanny in the revelation.

By nightfall he was fatigued, footsore, famishing. The thought of his wife and children urged him on. At last he found a

3

road which led him in what he knew to be
the right direction. It was as wide and
straight as a city street, yet it seemed untravelled. No fields bordered it, no dwelling anywhere. Not so much as the barking
of a dog suggested human habitation. The
black bodies of the trees formed a straight
wall on both sides, terminating on the horizon in a point, like a diagram in a lesson
in perspective. Overhead, as he looked up
through this rift in the wood, shone great
golden stars looking unfamiliar and grouped
in strange constellations. He was sure they
were arranged in some order which had a
secret and malign significance. The wood on
either side was full of singular noises, among
which—once, twice, and again—he distinctly
heard whispers in an unknown tongue.

His neck was in pain, and, lifting his hand
to it, he found it horribly swollen. He knew
that it had a circle of black where the rope
had bruised it. His eyes felt congested; he
could no longer close them. His tongue
was swollen with thirst; he relieved its
fever by thrusting it forward from between
his teeth into the cool air. How softly the
turf had carpeted the untravelled avenue—

he could no longer feel the roadway beneath his feet !

Doubtless, despite his suffering, he had fallen asleep while walking, for now he sees another scene—perhaps he has merely recovered from a delirium. He stands at the gate of his own home. All is as he left it, and all bright and beautiful in the morning sunshine. He must have travelled the entire night. As he pushes open the gate and passes up the wide white walk, he sees a flutter of female garments; his wife, looking fresh and cool and sweet, steps down from the veranda to meet him. At the bottom of the steps she stands waiting, with a smile of ineffable joy, an attitude of matchless grace and dignity. Ah, how beautiful she is ! He springs forward with extended arms. As he is about to clasp her, he feels a stunning blow upon the back of the neck ; a blinding white light blazes all about him, with a sound like the shock of a cannon— then all is darkness and silence !

Peyton Farquhar was dead ; his body, with a broken neck, swung gently from side to side beneath the timbers of the Owl Creek bridge.

Chickamauga

ONE sunny autumn afternoon a child strayed away from its rude home in a small field and entered a forest unobserved. It was happy in a new sense of freedom from control, happy in the opportunity of exploration and adventure ; for this child's spirit, in bodies of its ancestors, had for many thousands of years been trained to memorable feats of discovery and conquest—victories in battles whose critical moments were centuries, whose victors' camps were cities of hewn stone. From the cradle of its race it had conquered its way through two continents, and, passing a great sea, had penetrated a third, there to be born to war and dominion as a heritage.

The child was a boy, aged about six years, the son of a poor planter. In his younger

manhood the father had been a soldier, had
fought against naked savages, and followed
the flag of his country into the capital of
a civilized race to the far South. In the
peaceful life of a planter, the warrior-fire
survived ; once kindled, it is never extinguished. The man loved military books
and pictures, and the boy had understood
enough to make himself a wooden sword,
though even the eye of his father would
hardly have known it for what it was. This
weapon he now bore bravely, as became the
son of an heroic race, and, pausing now and
again in the sunny spaces of the forest,
assumed, with some exaggeration, the postures of aggression and defense that he had
been taught by the engraver's art. Made
reckless by the ease with which he overcame
invisible foes attempting to stay his advance,
he committed the common enough military
error of pushing the pursuit to a dangerous
extreme, until he found himself upon the
margin of a wide but shallow brook, whose
rapid waters barred his direct advance
against the flying foe that had crossed with
illogical ease. But the intrepid victor was
not to be baffled ; the spirit of the race

which had passed the great sea burned un-
conquerable in that small breast and would
not be denied. Finding a place where some
bowlders in the bed of the stream lay but a
step or a leap apart, he made his way across
and fell again upon the rear-guard of his
imaginary foe, putting all to the sword.

Now that the battle had been won, pru-
dence required that he withdraw to his base
of operations. Alas ! like many a mightier
conqueror, and like one, the mightiest, he
could not

> " curb the lust for war,
> Nor learn that tempted Fate will leave the loftiest
>   star."

Advancing from the bank of the creek,
he suddenly found himself confronted with
a new and more formidable enemy : in the
path that he was following, sat, bolt upright,
with ears erect and paws suspended before
it, a rabbit ! With a startled cry the child
turned and fled, he knew not in what direction, calling with inarticulate cries for his
mother, weeping, stumbling, his tender skin
cruelly torn by brambles, his little heart
beating hard with terror—breathless, blind
with tears—lost in the forest ! Then, for

more than an hour, he wandered with erring feet through the tangled undergrowth, till at last, overcome with fatigue, he lay down in a narrow space between two rocks, within a few yards of the stream, and, still grasping his toy sword, no longer a weapon but a companion, sobbed himself to sleep. The wood birds sang merrily above his head ; the squirrels, whisking their bravery of tail, ran barking from tree to tree, unconscious of the pity of it, and somewhere far away was a strange, muffled thunder, as if the partridges were drumming in celebration of nature's victory over the son of her immemorial enslavers. And back at the little plantation, where white men and black were hastily searching the fields and hedges in alarm, a mother's heart was breaking for her missing child.

Hours passed, and then the little sleeper rose to his feet. The chill of the evening was in his limbs, the fear of the gloom in his heart. But he had rested, and he no longer wept. With some blind instinct which impelled to action, he struggled through the undergrowth about him and came to a more open ground—on his right the brook, to the

left a gentle acclivity studded with infrequent trees; over all, the gathering gloom
of twilight.   A thin, ghostly mist rose along
the water.   It frightened and repelled him;
instead of recrossing, in the direction whence
he had come, he turned his back upon it,
and went forward toward the dark inclosing wood. Suddenly he saw before him a
strange moving object which he took to be
some large animal—a dog, a pig—he could
not name it; perhaps it was a bear. He
had seen pictures of bears, but knew of
nothing to their discredit, and had vaguely
wished to meet one.   But something in form
or movement of this object—something in
the awkwardness of its approach—told him
that it was not a bear, and curiosity was
stayed by fear. He stood still, and as it
came slowly on, gained courage every moment, for he saw that at least it had not the
long, menacing ears of the rabbit. Possibly
his impressionable mind was half conscious
of something familiar in its shambling, awk-
ward gait. Before it had approached near
enough to resolve his doubts, he saw that it
was followed by another and another. To
right and to left were many more; the

whole open space about him was alive with them—all moving forward toward the brook.

They were men. They crept upon their hands and knees. They used their hands only, dragging their legs. They used their knees only, their arms hanging idle at their sides. They strove to rise to their feet, but fell prone in the attempt. They did nothing naturally, and nothing alike, save only to advance foot by foot in the same direction. Singly, in pairs, and in little groups, they came on through the gloom, some halting now and again while others crept slowly past them, then resuming their movement. They came by dozens and by hundreds; as far on either hand as one could see in the deepening gloom they extended, and the black wood behind them appeared to be in-exhaustible. The very ground seemed in motion toward the creek. Occasionally one who had paused did not again go on, but lay motionless. He was dead. Some, paus-ing, made strange gestures with their hands, erected their arms and lowered them again, clasped their heads; spread their palms up-ward, as men are sometimes seen to do in public prayer.

Not all of this did the child note ; it is what would have been noted by an older observer ; he saw little but that these were men, yet crept like babes. Being men, they were not terrible, though unfamiliarly clad. He moved among them freely, going from one to another and peering into their faces with childish curiosity. All their faces were singularly white and many were streaked and gouted with red. Something in this—something too, perhaps, in their grotesque attitudes and movements—reminded him of the painted clown whom he had seen last summer in the circus, and he laughed as he watched them. But on and ever on they crept, these maimed and bleeding men, as heedless as he of the dramatic contrast between his laughter and their own ghastly gravity. To him it was a merry spectacle. He had seen his father's negroes creep upon their hands and knees for his amusement— had ridden them so, "making believe" they were his horses. He now approached one of these crawling figures from behind and with an agile movement mounted it astride. The man sank upon his breast, recovered, flung the small boy fiercely to the ground as an unbroken colt might have done, then turned upon him a face that lacked a lower jaw—from the upper teeth to the throat was a great red gap fringed with hanging shreds of flesh and splinters of bone. The unnatural prominence of nose, the absence of chin, the fierce eyes, gave this man the appearance of a great bird of prey crimsoned in throat and breast by the blood of its quarry. The man rose to his knees, the child to his feet. The man shook his fist at the child; the child, terrified at last, ran to a tree near by, got upon the farther side of it, and took a more serious view of the situation. And so the clumsy multitude dragged itself slowly and painfully along in hideous pantomime—moved forward down the slope like a swarm of great black beetles, with never a sound of going—in silence profound, absolute.

Instead of darkening, the haunted landscape began to brighten. Through the belt of trees beyond the brook shone a strange red light, the trunks and branches of the trees making a black lacework against it. It struck the creeping figures and gave them monstrous shadows, which caricatured their

movements on the lit grass. It fell upon
their faces, touching their whiteness with
a ruddy tinge, accentuating the stains with
which so many of them were freaked and
maculated.   It sparkled on buttons and bits
of metal in their clothing. Instinctively the
child turned toward the growing splendor
and moved down the slope with his horrible
companions ; in a few moments, had passed
the foremost of the throng—not much of a
feat, considering his advantages. He placed
himself in the lead, his wooden sword still in
hand, and solemnly directed the march, con-
forming his pace to theirs and occasionally
turning as if to see that his forces did not
straggle. Surely such a leader never before
had such a following.

Scattered about upon the ground now
slowly narrowing by the encroachment of
this awful march to water, were certain arti-
cles to which, in the leader's mind, were
coupled no significant associations : an occasional blanket, tightly rolled lengthwise,
doubled and the ends bound together with a
string ; a heavy knapsack here, and there a
broken rifle—such things, in short, as are
found in the rear of retreating troops, the

"spoor" of men flying from their hunters. Everywhere near the creek, which here had a margin of lowland, the earth was trodden into mud by the feet of men and horses. An observer of better experience in the use of his eyes would have noticed that these footprints pointed in both directions; the ground had been twice passed over—in advance and in retreat. A few hours before, these desperate, stricken men, with their more fortunate and now distant comrades, had penetrated the forest in thousands. Their successive battalions, breaking into swarms and re-forming in lines, had passed the child on every side—had almost trodden on him as he slept. The rustle and murmur of their march had not awakened him. Almost within a stone's throw of where he lay they had fought a battle; but all unheard by him were the roar of the musketry, the shock of the cannon, "the thunder of the captains and the shouting." He had slept through it all, grasping his little wooden sword with perhaps a tighter clutch in unconscious sympathy with his martial environment, but as heedless of the grandeur of the struggle as the dead who died to make the glory.

The fire beyond the belt of woods on the farther side of the creek, reflected to earth from the canopy of its own smoke, was now suffusing the whole landscape. It transformed the sinuous line of mist to the vapor of gold. The water gleamed with dashes of red, and red, too, were many of the stones protruding above the surface. But that was blood; the less desperately wounded had stained them in crossing. On them, too, the child now crossed with eager steps; he was going to the fire. As he stood upon the farther bank, he turned about to look at the companions of his march. The advance was arriving at the creek. The stronger had already drawn themselves to the brink and plunged their faces into the flood. Three or four who lay without motion appeared to have no heads. At this the child's eyes expanded with wonder; even his hospitable understanding could not accept a phenomenon implying such vitality as that. After slaking their thirst, these men had not had the strength to back away from the water, nor to keep their heads above it. They were drowned. In rear of these, the open spaces of the forest showed the leader as many formless figures of his grim command as at first;

but not nearly so many were in motion. He waved his cap for their encouragement and smilingly pointed with his weapon in the direction of the guiding light—a pillar of fire to this strange exodus.

Confident of the fidelity of his forces, he now entered the belt of woods, passed through it easily in the red illumination, climbed a fence, ran across a field, turning now and again to coquet with his responsive shadow, and so approached the blazing ruin of a dwelling. Desolation everywhere. In all the wide glare not a living thing was visible. He cared nothing for that ; the spectacle pleased, and he danced with glee in imitation of the wavering flames. He ran about collecting fuel, but every object that he found was too heavy for him to cast in from the distance to which the heat limited his approach. In despair he flung in his sword—a surrender to the superior forces of nature. His military career was at an end.

Shifting his position, his eyes fell upon some outbuildings which had an oddly familiar appearance, as if he had dreamed of them. He stood considering them with wonder, when suddenly the entire plantation, with its inclosing forest, seemed to turn as if upon a pivot. His little world swung half around ; the points of the compass were reversed. He recognized the blazing building as his own home !

For a moment he stood stupefied by the power of the revelation, then ran with stumbling feet, making a half-circuit of the ruin. There, conspicuous in the light of the conflagration, lay the dead body of a woman— the white face turned upward, the hands thrown out and clutched full of grass, the clothing deranged, the long dark hair in tangles and full of clotted blood. The greater part of the forehead was torn away, and from the jagged hole the brain protruded, overflowing the temple, a frothy mass of gray, crowned with clusters of crimson bubbles—the work of a shell.

The child moved his little hands, making wild, uncertain gestures. He uttered a series of inarticulate and indescribable cries— something between the chattering of an ape and the gobbling of a turkey—a startling, soulless, unholy sound, the language of a devil. The child was a deaf-mute.

Then he stood motionless, with quivering lips, looking down upon the wreck.

A Son of the Gods

A STUDY IN THE HISTORICAL PRESENT TENSE

A BREEZY day and a sunny landscape. An open country to right and left and forward ; behind, a wood. In the edge of this wood, facing the open but not venturing into it, long lines of troops halted. The wood is alive with them, and full of confused noises—the occasional rattle of wheels as a battery of artillery goes into position to cover the advance ; the hum and murmur of the soldiers talking ; a sound of innumerable feet in the dry leaves that strew the interspaces among the trees ; hoarse commands of officers. Detached groups of horsemen are well in front—not altogether exposed—many of them intently regarding the crest of a hill a mile away in the direction of the interrupted advance. For this powerful army, moving in battle order through a forest, has met with a formidable obstacle—the open country. The crest of that gentle hill a mile away has a sinister look ; it says, Beware ! Along it runs a stone wall extending to left and right a great distance. Behind the wall is a hedge ; behind the hedge are seen the tops of trees in rather straggling order. Among the trees —what ? It is necessary to know.

Yesterday, and for many days and nights previously, we were fighting somewhere ; always there was cannonading, with occasional keen rattlings of musketry, mingled with cheers, our own or the enemy's, we seldom knew, attesting some temporary advantage. This morning at daybreak the enemy was gone. We have moved forward across his earthworks, across which we have so often vainly attempted to move before, through the débris of his abandoned camps, among the graves of his fallen, into the woods beyond.

How curiously we regarded everything ! how odd it all seemed ! Nothing appeared quite familiar ; the most commonplace objects—an old saddle, a splintered wheel, a forgotten canteen—everything related something of the mysterious personality of those strange men who had been killing us. The soldier never becomes wholly familiar with the conception of his foes as men like himself; he cannot divest himself of the feeling that they are another order of beings, differently conditioned, in an environment not altogether of the earth. The smallest vestiges of them rivet his attention and engage his interest. He thinks of them as inaccessible; and, catching an unexpected glimpse of them, they appear farther away, and therefore larger, than they really are—like objects in a fog. He is somewhat in awe of them.

From the edge of the wood leading up the acclivity are the tracks of horses and wheels—the wheels of cannon. The yellow grass is beaten down by the feet of infantry. Clearly they have passed this way in thousands; they have not withdrawn by the country roads. This is significant—it is the difference between retiring and retreating.

That group of horsemen is our commander, his staff, and escort. He is facing the distant crest, holding his field-glass

against his eyes with both hands, his elbows needlessly elevated. It is a fashion ;
it seems to dignify the act ; we are all addicted to it. Suddenly he lowers the glass
and says a few words to those about him.
Two or three aides detach themselves from
the group and canter away into the woods,
along the lines in each direction. We did
not hear his words, but we knew them :
" Tell General X. to send forward the skirmish line."   Those of us who have been out
of place resume our positions ; the men resting at ease straighten themselves, and the
ranks are re-formed without a command.
Some of us staff officers dismount and look
at our saddle girths ; those already on the
ground remount.

Galloping rapidly along in the edge of
the open ground comes a young officer on
a snow-white horse. His saddle blanket is
scarlet. What a fool ! No one who has
ever been in battle but remembers how naturally every rifle turns toward the man on a
white horse ; no one but has observed how
a bit of red enrages the bull of battle. That
such colors are fashionable in military life
must be accepted as the most astonishing

of all the phenomena of human vanity. They would seem to have been devised to increase the death-rate.

This young officer is in full uniform, as if on parade. He is all agleam with bullion—a blue-and-gold edition of the Poetry of War. A wave of derisive laughter runs abreast of him all along the line. But how handsome he is !—with what careless grace he sits his horse !

He reins up within a respectful distance of the corps commander and salutes. The old soldier nods familiarly ; he evidently knows him. A brief colloquy between them is going on ; the young man seems to be preferring some request which the elder one is indisposed to grant. Let us ride a little nearer. Ah ! too late—it is ended. The young officer salutes again, wheels his horse, and rides straight toward the crest of the hill. He is deadly pale.

A thin line of skirmishers, the men deployed at six paces or so apart, now pushes from the wood into the open. The commander speaks to his bugler, who claps his instrument to his lips. *Tra-la-la ! Tra-la-la!* The skirmishers halt in their tracks.

Meantime the young horseman has advanced a hundred yards. He is riding at a walk, straight up the long slope, with never a turn of the head. How glorious! Gods! what would we not give to be in his place—with his soul! He does not draw his sabre; his right hand hangs easily at his side. The breeze catches the plume in his hat and flutters it smartly. The sunshine rests upon his shoulder-straps, lovingly, like a visible benediction. Straight on he rides. Ten thousand pairs of eyes are fixed upon him with an intensity that he can hardly fail to feel; ten thousand hearts keep quick time to the inaudible hoof-beats of his snowy steed. He is not alone—he draws all souls after him; we are but "dead men all." But we remember that we laughed! On and on, straight for the hedge-lined wall, he rides. Not a look backward. Oh, if he would but turn—if he could but see the love, the adoration, the atonement!

Not a word is spoken; the populous depths of the forest still murmur with their unseen and unseeing swarm, but all along the fringe there is silence absolute. The burly commander is an equestrian statue of himself. The mounted staff officers, their field glasses up, are motionless all. The line of battle in the edge of the wood stands at a new kind of "attention," each man in the attitude in which he was caught by the consciousness of what is going on. All these hardened and impenitent man killers, to whom death in its awfulest forms is a fact familiar to their every-day observation ; who sleep on hills trembling with the thunder of great guns, dine in the midst of streaming missiles, and play at cards among the dead faces of their dearest friends—all are watching with suspended breath and beating hearts the outcome of an act involving the life of one man. Such is the magnetism of courage and devotion.

If now you should turn your head you would see a simultaneous movement among the spectators—a start, as if they had received an electric shock—and looking forward again to the now distant horseman you would see that he has in that instant altered his direction and is riding at an angle to his former course. The spectators suppose the sudden deflection to be caused by a shot, perhaps a wound ; but take this field glass and you will observe that he is riding toward a break in the wall and hedge. He means, if not killed, to ride through and overlook the country beyond.

You are not to forget the nature of this man's act; it is not permitted to you to think of it as an instance of bravado, nor, on the other hand, a needless sacrifice of self. If the enemy has not retreated he is in force on that ridge. The investigator will encounter nothing less than a line of battle; there is no need of pickets, videttes, skirmishers, to give warning of our approach; our attacking lines will be visible, conspicuous, exposed to an artillery fire that will shave the ground the moment they break from cover, and for half the distance to a sheet of rifle bullets in which nothing can live. In short, if the enemy is there, it would be madness to attack him in front; he must be manœuvred out by the immemorial plan of threatening his line of communication, as necessary to his existence as to the diver at the bottom of the sea his air tube. But how ascertain if the enemy is there? There is but one way,—somebody must go and see. The natural and customary thing to do is to send forward a line of skirmishers. But in this case they will answer in the affirmative with all their lives ; the enemy, crouching in double ranks behind the stone wall and in cover of the hedge, will wait until it is possible to count each assailant's teeth. At the first volley a half of the questioning line will fall, the other half before it can accomplish the pre-destined retreat. What a price to pay for gratified curiosity ! At what a dear rate an army must sometimes purchase knowledge ! " Let me pay all," says this gallant man—this military Christ !

There is no hope except the hope against hope that the crest is clear. True, he might prefer capture to death. So long as he advances, the line will not fire — why should it ? He can safely ride into the hostile ranks and become a prisoner of war. But this would defeat his object. It would not answer our question ; it is necessary either that he return unharmed or be shot to death before our eyes. Only so shall we know how to act. If captured—why, that might have been done by a half-dozen stragglers.

Now begins an extraordinary contest of in-

tellect between a man and an army. Our
horseman, now within a quarter of a mile of
the crest, suddenly wheels to the left and gal-
lops in a direction parallel to it. He has
caught sight of his antagonist; he knows all.
Some slight advantage of ground has enabled
him to overlook a part of the line. If he
were here, he could tell us in words. But that
is now hopeless; he must make the best use
of the few minutes of life remaining to him,
by compelling the enemy himself to tell us as.
much and as plainly as possible—which, naturally, that discreet power is reluctant to do.
Not a rifleman in those crouching ranks, not
a cannoneer at those masked and shotted
guns, but knows the needs of the situation,
the imperative duty of forbearance. Besides,
there has been time enough to forbid them
all to fire. True, a single rifle-shot might
drop him and be no great disclosure. But
firing is infectious—and see how rapidly he
moves, with never a pause except as he
whirls his horse about to take a new direction, never directly backward toward us,
never directly forward toward his executioners. All this is visible through the glass;
it seems occurring within pistol-shot; we

see all but the enemy, whose presence, whose thoughts, whose motives we infer. To the unaided eye there is nothing but a black figure on a white horse, tracing slow zigzags against the slope of a distant hill—so slowly they seem almost to creep.

Now—the glass again—he has tired of his failure, or sees his error, or has gone mad; he is dashing directly forward at the wall, as if to take it at a leap, hedge and all! One moment only and he wheels right about and is speeding like the wind straight down the slope—toward his friends, toward his death! Instantly the wall is topped with a fierce roll of smoke for a distance of hundreds of yards to right and left. This is as instantly dissipated by the wind, and before the rattle of the rifles reaches us, he is down. No, he recovers his seat; he has but pulled his horse upon its haunches. They are up and away! A tremendous cheer bursts from our ranks, relieving the insupportable tension of our feelings. And the horse and its rider? Yes, they are up and away. Away, indeed—they are making directly to our left, parallel to the now steadily blazing and smoking wall. The rattle of the musketry is continuous, and

every bullet's target is that courageous
heart.

Suddenly a great bank of white smoke
pushes upward from behind the wall. Another and another—a dozen roll up before
the thunder of the explosions and the humming of the missiles reach our ears, and the
missiles themselves come bounding through
clouds of dust into our covert, knocking
over here and there a man and causing a
temporary distraction, a passing thought of
self.

The dust drifts away. Incredible !—that
enchanted horse and rider have passed a
ravine and are climbing another slope to un-
veil another conspiracy of silence, to thwart
the will of another armed host. Another moment and that crest too is in eruption. The
horse rears and strikes the air with its forefeet. They are down at last. But look
again—the man has detached himself from
the dead animal. He stands erect, motionless, holding his sabre in his right hand
straight above his head. His face is toward
us. Now he lowers his hand to a level with
his face and moves it outward, the blade of
the sabre describing a downward curve. It

is a sign to us, to the world, to posterity. It is a hero's salute to death and history.

Again the spell is broken; our men attempt to cheer; they are choking with emotion; they utter hoarse, discordant cries; they clutch their weapons and press tumultuously forward into the open. The skirmishers, without orders, against orders, are going forward at a keen run, like hounds unleashed. Our cannon speak and the enemy's now open in full chorus; to right and left as far as we can see, the distant crest, seeming now so near, erects its towers of cloud, and the great shot pitch roaring down among our moving masses. Flag after flag of ours emerges from the wood, line after line sweeps forth, catching the sunlight on its burnished arms. The rear battalions alone are in obedience; they preserve their proper distance from the insurgent front.

The commander has not moved. He now removes his field glass from his eyes and glances to the right and left. He sees the human current flowing on either side of him and his huddled escort, like tide waves parted by a rock. Not a sign of feeling in his face ; he is thinking. Again he directs his eyes forward ; they slowly traverse that malign and awful crest. He addresses a calm word to his bugler. *Tra-la-la ! Tra-la-la !* The injunction has an imperiousness which enforces it. It is repeated by all the bugles of all the subordinate commanders ; the sharp metallic notes assert themselves above the hum of the advance, and penetrate the sound of the cannon. To halt is to withdraw. The colors move slowly back ; the lines face about and sullenly follow, bearing their wounded ; the skirmishers return, gathering up the dead.

Ah, those many, many needless dead ! That great soul whose beautiful body is lying over yonder, so conspicuous against the sere hillside—could it not have been spared the bitter consciousness of a vain devotion ? Would one exception have marred too much the pitiless perfection of the divine, eternal plan ?

One of the Missing

I

JEROME SEARING, a private soldier of General Sherman's army, then confronting the enemy at and about Kenesaw Mountain, Georgia, turned his back upon a small group of officers, with whom he had been talking in low tones, stepped across a light line of earthworks, and disappeared in a forest. None of the men in line behind the works had said a word to him, nor had he so much as nodded to them in passing, but all who saw understood that this brave man had been intrusted with some perilous duty. Jerome Searing, though a private, did not serve in the ranks; he was detailed for service at division headquarters, being borne upon the rolls as an orderly. "Orderly" is a word covering a multitude

of duties.   An orderly may be a messenger,
a clerk, an officer's servant—anything.   He
may perform services for which no provision
is made in orders and army regulations.
Their nature may depend upon his aptitude,
upon favor, upon accident.   Private Searing, an incomparable marksman, young,—it
is surprising how young we all were in those
days,—hardy, intelligent, and insensible to
fear, was a scout.   The general commanding his division was not content to obey orders blindly without knowing what was in
his front, even when his command was not
on detached service, but formed a fraction
of the line of the army ; nor was he satisfied
to receive his knowledge of his *vis-a-vis*
through the customary channels ; he wanted
to know more than he was apprised of by
the corps commander and the collisions of
pickets and skirmishers.   Hence Jerome
Searing—with his extraordinary daring, his
woodcraft, his sharp eyes, and truthful
tongue.   On this occasion his instructions
were simple : to get as near the enemy's
lines as possible and learn all that he could.

In a few moments he had arrived at the
picket-line, the men on duty there lying in

groups of two and four behind little banks of earth scooped out of the slight depression in which they lay, their rifles protruding from the green boughs with which they had masked their small defenses. The forest extended without a break toward the front, so solemn and silent that only by an effort of the imagination could it be conceived as populous with armed men, alert and vigilant —a forest formidable with possibilities of battle. Pausing a moment in one of these rifle-pits to apprise the men of his intention, Searing crept stealthily forward on his hands and knees and was soon lost to view in a dense thicket of underbrush.

"That is the last of him," said one of the men; "I wish I had his rifle; those fellows will hurt some of us with it."

Searing crept on, taking advantage of every accident of ground and growth to give himself better cover. His eyes penetrated everywhere, his ears took note of every sound. He stilled his breathing, and at the cracking of a twig beneath his knee stopped his progress and hugged the earth. It was slow work, but not tedious; the danger made it exciting, but by no physical signs was the excitement manifest. His pulse was as regular, his nerves were as steady, as if he were trying to trap a sparrow.

"It seems a long time," he thought, "but I cannot have come very far; I am still alive."

He smiled at his own method of estimating distance, and crept forward. A moment later he suddenly flattened himself upon the earth and lay motionless, minute after minute. Through a narrow opening in the bushes he had caught sight of a small mound of yellow clay—one of the enemy's rifle-pits. After some little time he cautiously raised his head, inch by inch, then his body upon his hands, spread out on each side of him, all the while intently regarding the hillock of clay. In another moment he was upon his feet, rifle in hand, striding rapidly forward with little attempt at concealment. He had rightly interpreted the signs, whatever they were; the enemy was gone.

To assure himself beyond a doubt before going back to report upon so important a matter, Searing pushed forward across the line of abandoned pits, running from cover

to cover in the more open forest, his eyes
vigilant to discover possible stragglers. He
came to the edge of a plantation—one of
those forlorn, deserted homesteads of the last
years of the war, upgrown with brambles,
ugly with broken fences, and desolate with
vacant buildings having blank apertures in
place of doors and windows. After a keen
reconnoissance from the safe seclusion of a
clump of young pines, Searing ran lightly
across a field and through an orchard to a
small structure which stood apart from the
other farm buildings, on a slight elevation,
which he thought would enable him to overlook a large scope of country in the direction
that he supposed the enemy to have taken
in withdrawing. This building, which had
originally consisted of a single room, elevated
upon four posts about ten feet high, was now
little more than a roof ; the floor had fallen
away, the joists and planks loosely piled on
the ground below or resting on end at various angles, not wholly torn from their fast-
enings above. The supporting posts were
themselves no longer vertical. It looked as
if the whole edifice would go down at the
touch of a finger. Concealing himself in the

débris of joists and flooring, Searing looked across the open ground between his point of view and a spur of Kenesaw Mountain, a half-mile away. A road leading up and across this spur was crowded with troops—the rear-guard of the retiring enemy, their gun barrels gleaming in the morning sunlight.

Searing had now learned all that he could hope to know. It was his duty to return to his own command with all possible speed and report his discovery. But the gray column of infantry toiling up the mountain road was singularly tempting. His rifle—an ordinary "Springfield," but fitted with a globe sight and hair-trigger—would easily send its ounce and a quarter of lead hissing into their midst. That would probably not affect the duration and result of the war, but it is the business of a soldier to kill. It is also his pleasure if he is a good soldier. Searing cocked his rifle and "set" the trigger.

But it was decreed from the beginning of time that Private Searing was not to murder anybody that bright summer morning, nor was the Confederate retreat to be announced by him. For countless ages events had been so matching themselves together in that wondrous mosaic to some parts of which, dimly discernible, we give the name of history, that the acts which he had in will would have marred the harmony of the pattern.

Some twenty-five years previously the Power charged with the execution of the work according to the design had provided against that mischance by causing the birth of a certain male child in a little village at the foot of the Carpathian Mountains, had carefully reared it, supervised its education, directed its desires into a military channel, and in due time made it an officer of artillery. By the concurrence of an infinite number of favoring influences and their preponderance over an infinite number of opposing ones, this officer of artillery had been made to commit a breach of discipline and fly from his native country to avoid punishment. He had been directed to New Orleans (instead of New York), where a recruiting officer awaited him on the wharf. He was enlisted and promoted, and things were so ordered that he now commanded a Confederate battery some two miles along the line from where Jerome Searing, the

Federal scout, stood cocking his rifle. Nothing had been neglected—at every step in the progress of both these men's lives, and in the lives of their contemporaries and ancestors, and in the lives of the contemporaries of their ancestors, the right thing had been done to bring about the desired result. Had anything in all this vast concatenation been overlooked, Private Searing might have fired on the retreating Confederates that morning, and would perhaps have missed. As it fell out, a Confederate captain of artillery, having nothing better to do while awaiting his turn to pull out and be off, amused himself by sighting a field-piece obliquely to his right at what he took to be some Federal officers on the crest of a hill, and discharged it. The shot flew high of its mark.

As Jerome Searing drew back the hammer of his rifle, and, with his eyes upon the distant Confederates, considered where he could plant his shot with the best hope of making a widow or an orphan or a childless mother—perhaps all three, for Private Searing, although he had repeatedly refused promotion, was not without a certain kind of ambition,—he heard a rushing sound in the air, like that made by the wings of a great bird swooping down upon its prey. More quickly than he could apprehend the gradation, it increased to a hoarse and horrible roar, as the missile that made it sprang at him out of the sky, striking with a deafening impact one of the posts supporting the confusion of timbers above him, smashing it into matchwood, and bringing down the crazy edifice with a loud clatter, in clouds of blinding dust !

II

Lieutenant Adrian Searing, in command of the picket-guard on that part of the line through which his brother Jerome had passed on his mission, sat with attentive ears in his breastwork behind the line. Not the faintest sound escaped him ; the cry of a bird, the barking of a squirrel, the noise of the wind among the pines—all were anxiously noted by his overstrained sense. Suddenly, directly in front of his line, he heard a faint, confused rumble, like the clatter of a falling building translated by distance. At the same moment an officer approached him on foot from the rear and saluted.

" Lieutenant," said the aide, " the colonel directs you to move forward your line and feel the enemy if you find him. If not, continue the advance until directed to halt. There is reason to think that the enemy has retreated."

The lieutenant nodded and said nothing ; the other officer retired. In a moment the men, apprised of their duty by the non-commissioned officers in low tones, had deployed from their rifle-pits and were moving forward in skirmishing order, with set teeth and beating hearts. The lieutenant mechanically looked at his watch. Six o'clock and eighteen minutes.

III

When Jerome Searing recovered consciousness, he did not at once understand what had occurred. It was, indeed, some time before he opened his eyes. For a while he believed that he had died and been buried, and he tried to recall some portions of the burial service. He thought that his wife was kneeling upon his grave, adding her weight to that of the earth upon his breast. The two of them, widow and earth, had crushed his coffin. Unless the children should persuade her to go home, he would not much longer be able to breathe. He felt a sense of wrong. "I cannot speak to her," he thought; "the dead have no voice; and if I open my eyes I shall get them full of earth."

He opened his eyes—a great expanse of blue sky, rising from a fringe of the tops of trees. In the foreground, shutting out some of the trees, a high, dun mound, angular in outline and crossed by an intricate, pattern-less system of straight lines; in the centre a small bright ring of metal—the whole an immeasurable distance away—a distance so inconceivably great that it fatigued him, and he closed his eyes. The moment that he did so he was conscious of an insufferable light. A sound was in his ears like the low, rhythmic thunder of a distant sea breaking in successive waves upon the beach, and out of this noise, seeming a part of it, or possibly coming from beyond it, and intermingled with its ceaseless undertone, came the artic-ulate words: "Jerome Searing, you are caught like a rat in a trap—in a trap, trap, trap."

Suddenly there fell a great silence, a black darkness, an infinite tranquillity, and Jerome Searing, perfectly conscious of his rathood, and well assured of the trap that he was in, remembering all and nowise alarmed, again opened his eyes to reconnoitre, to note the strength of his enemy, to plan his defense.

He was caught in a reclining posture, his back firmly supported by a solid beam. Another lay across his breast, but he had been able to shrink a little away from it so that it no longer oppressed him, though it was immovable. A brace joining it at an angle had wedged him against a pile of boards on his left, fastening the arm on that side. His legs, slightly parted and straight along the ground, were covered upward to the knees with a mass of débris which towered above his narrow horizon. His head was as rigidly fixed as in a vice ; he could move his eyes, his chin—no more. Only his right arm was partly free. "You must help us out of this," he said to it. But he could not get it from under the heavy timber athwart his chest, nor move it outward more than six inches at the elbow.

Searing was not seriously injured, nor did

he suffer pain. A smart rap on the head from a flying fragment of the splintered post, incurred simultaneously with the frightfully sudden shock to the nervous system, had momentarily dazed him. His term of unconsciousness, including the period of recovery, during which he had had the strange fancies, had probably not exceeded a few seconds, for the dust of the wreck had not wholly cleared away as he began an intelligent survey of the situation.

With his partly free right hand he now tried to get hold of the beam which lay across, but not quite against, his breast. In no way could he do so. He was unable to depress the shoulder so as to push the elbow beyond that edge of the timber which was nearest his knees ; failing in that, he could not raise the forearm and hand to grasp the beam. The brace that made an angle with it downward and backward prevented him from doing anything in that direction, and between it and his body the space was not half as wide as the length of his forearm. Obviously he could not get his hand under the beam nor over it ; the hand could not, in fact, touch it at all. Having demonstrated his inability, he desisted, and began to think if he could reach any of the débris piled upon his legs.

In surveying the mass with a view to determining that point, his attention was arrested by what seemed to be a ring of shining metal immediately in front of his eyes. It appeared to him at first to surround some perfectly black substance, and it was somewhat more than a half-inch in diameter. It suddenly occurred to his mind that the blackness was simply shadow, and that the ring was in fact the muzzle of his rifle protruding from the pile of débris. He was not long in satisfying himself that this was so—if it was a satisfaction. By closing either eye he could look a little way along the barrel—to the point where it was hidden by the rubbish that held it. He could see the one side, with the corresponding eye, at apparently the same angle as the other side with the other eye. Looking with the right eye, the weapon seemed to be directed at a point to the left of his head, and *vice versa*. He was unable to see the upper surface of the barrel, but could see the under surface of the stock at a slight angle. The piece was, in

fact, aimed at the exact centre of his forehead.

In the perception of this circumstance, in
the recollection that just previously to the
mischance of which this uncomfortable situation was the result, he had cocked the rifle
and set the trigger so that a touch would
discharge it, Private Searing was affected
with a feeling of uneasiness. But that was as
far as possible from fear ; he was a brave
man, somewhat familiar with the aspect of
rifles from that point of view, and of cannon
too ; and now he recalled, with something
like amusement, an incident of his experience at the storming of Missionary Ridge,
where, walking up to one of the enemy's
embrasures from which he had seen a heavy
gun throw charge after charge of grape
among the assailants, he thought for a moment that the piece had been withdrawn ; he
could see nothing in the opening but a
brazen circle. What that was he had understood just in time to step aside as it
pitched another peck of iron down that
swarming slope. To face firearms is one of
the commonest incidents in a soldier's life
—firearms, too, with malevolent eyes blaz-

ing behind them. That is what a soldier is for. Still, Private Searing did not altogether relish the situation, and turned away his eyes.

After groping, aimless, with his right hand for a time, he made an ineffectual attempt to release his left. Then he tried to disengage his head, the fixity of which was the more annoying from his ignorance of what held it. Next he tried to free his feet, but while exerting the powerful muscles of his legs for that purpose it occurred to him that a disturbance of the rubbish which held them might discharge the rifle; how it could have endured what had already befallen it he could not understand, although memory assisted him with various instances in point. One in particular he recalled, in which, in a moment of mental abstraction, he had clubbed his rifle and beaten out another gentleman's brains, observing afterward that the weapon which he had been diligently swinging by the muzzle was loaded, capped, and at full cock—knowledge of which circumstance would doubtless have cheered his antagonist to longer endurance. He had always smiled in recalling that blunder of his " green and salad days " as a soldier, but now he did not smile. He turned his eyes again to the muzzle of the rifle, and for a moment fancied that it had moved ; it seemed somewhat nearer.

Again he looked away. The tops of the distant trees beyond the bounds of the plantation interested him : he had not before observed how light and feathery they were, ˙nor how darkly blue the sky was, even among their branches, where they somewhat paled it with their green ; above him it appeared almost black. " It will be uncomfortably hot here," he thought, "as the day advances. I wonder which way I am looking."

Judging by such shadows as he could see, he decided that his face was due north ; he would at least not have the sun in his eyes, and north—well, that was toward his wife and children.

" Bah ! " he exclaimed aloud, " what have they to do with it ? "

He closed his eyes. " As I can't get out I may as well go to sleep. The rebels are gone, and some of our fellows are sure to stray out here foraging. They 'll find me."

But he did not sleep. Gradually he became sensible of a pain in his forehead—a dull ache, hardly perceptible at first, but growing more and more uncomfortable. He opened his eyes and it was gone—closed them and it returned. " The devil ! " he said, irrelevantly, and stared again at the sky. He heard the singing of birds, the strange metallic note of the meadow lark, suggesting the clash of vibrant blades. He fell into pleasant memories of his childhood, played again with his brother and sister, raced across the fields, shouting to alarm the sedentary larks, entered the sombre forest beyond, and with timid steps followed the faint path to Ghost Rock, standing at last with audible heart-throbs before the Dead Man's Cave and seeking to penetrate its awful mystery. For the first time he observed that the opening of the haunted cavern was encircled by a ring of metal. Then all else vanished and left him gazing into the barrel of his rifle as before. But whereas before it had seemed nearer, it now seemed an inconceivable distance away, and all the more sinister for that. He cried out, and, startled by something in his own voice—the note of fear—lied to himself in denial : " If I don't sing out I may stay here till I die."

He now made no further attempt to evade the menacing stare of the gun barrel. If he turned away his eyes an instant, it was to look for assistance (although he could not see the ground on either side the ruin), and he permitted them to return, obedient to the imperative fascination. If he closed them, it was from weariness, and instantly the poignant pain in his forehead—the prophecy and menace of the bullet—forced him to reopen them.

The tension of nerve and brain was too severe ; nature came to his relief with intervals of unconsciousness. Reviving from one of these, he became sensible of a sharp, smarting pain in his right hand, and when he worked his fingers together, or rubbed his palm with them, he could feel that they were wet and slippery. He could not see the hand, but he knew the sensation ; it was running blood. In his delirium he had beaten it against the jagged fragments of the wreck, had clutched it full of splinters. He resolved that he would meet his fate more manly. He was a plain, common sol-

dier, had no religion and not much philoso-
phy ; he could not die like a hero, with
great and wise last words, even if there were
someone to hear them, but he could die
" game," and he would. But if he could
only know when to expect the shot !

Some rats which had probably inhabited
the shed came sneaking and scampering
about. One of them mounted the pile of débris that held the rifle ; another followed
and another. Searing regarded them at first
with indifference, then with friendly interest ;
then, as the thought flashed into his bewil-
dered mind that they might touch the trigger
of his rifle, he screamed at them to go away.
" It is no business of yours," he cried.

The creatures left ; they would return
later, attack his face, gnaw away his nose,
cut his throat—he knew that, but he hoped
by that time to be dead.

Nothing could now unfix his gaze from
the little ring of metal with its black inte-
rior. The pain in his forehead was fierce
and incessant. He felt it gradually penetrating the brain more and more deeply,
until at last its progress was arrested by the
wood at the back of his head. It grew

momentarily more insufferable : he began
wantonly beating his lacerated hand against
the splinters again to counteract that horrible ache. It seemed to throb with a slow,
regular recurrence, each pulsation sharper
than the preceding, and sometimes he cried
out, thinking he felt the fatal bullet. No
thoughts of home, of wife and children, of
country, of glory. The whole record of
memory was effaced. The world had passed
away—not a vestige remained. Here in
this confusion of timbers and boards is the
sole universe. Here is immortality in time
—each pain an everlasting life. The throbs
tick off eternities.

Jerome Searing, the man of courage, the
formidable enemy, the strong, resolute warrior, was as pale as a ghost. His jaw was
fallen ; his eyes protruded ; he trembled in
every fibre ; a cold sweat bathed his entire
body ; he screamed with fear. He was not
insane—he was terrified.

In groping about with his torn and bleeding hand he seized at last a strip of board,
and, pulling, felt it give way. It lay parallel with his body, and by bending his
elbow as much as the contracted space would

permit, he could draw it a few inches at a time. Finally it was altogether loosened from the wreckage covering his legs; he could lift it clear of the ground its whole length. A great hope came into his mind : perhaps he could work it upward, that is to say backward, far enough to lift the end and push aside the rifle ; or, if that were too tightly wedged, so place the strip of board as to deflect the bullet. With this object he passed it backward inch by inch, hardly daring to breathe lest that act somehow defeat his intent, and more than ever unable to remove his eyes from the rifle, which might perhaps now hasten to improve its waning opportunity. Something at least had been gained : in the occupation of his mind in this attempt at self-defense he was less sensible of the pain in his head and had ceased to scream. But he was still dreadfully frightened and his teeth rattled like castanets.

The strip of board ceased to move to the suasion of his hand. He tugged at it with all his strength, changed the direction of its length all he could, but it had met some extended obstruction behind him, and the end in front was still too far away to clear the pile of débris and reach the muzzle of the gun. It extended, indeed, nearly as far as the trigger guard, which, uncovered by the rubbish, he could imperfectly see with his right eye. He tried to break the strip with his hand, but had no leverage. Perceiving his defeat, all his terror returned, augmented tenfold. The black aperture of the rifle appeared to threaten a sharper and more imminent death in punishment of his rebellion. The track of the bullet through his head ached with an intenser anguish. He began to tremble again.

Suddenly he became composed. His tremor subsided. He clenched his teeth and drew down his eyebrows. He had not exhausted his means of defense ; a new design had shaped itself in his mind—another plan of battle. Raising the front end of the strip of board, he carefully pushed it forward through the wreckage at the side of the rifle until it pressed against the trigger guard. Then he moved the end slowly outward until he could feel that it had cleared it, then, closing his eyes, thrust it against the trigger with all his strength ! There was no explosion ; the rifle had been discharged as it dropped from his hand when the building fell. But Jerome Searing was dead.

IV

A line of Federal skirmishers swept across the plantation toward the mountain. They passed on both sides of the wrecked building, observing nothing. At a short distance in their rear came their commander, Lieutenant Adrian Searing. He casts his eyes curiously upon the ruin and sees a dead body half buried in boards and timbers. It is so covered with dust that its clothing is Confederate gray. Its face is yellowish white ; the cheeks are fallen in, the temples sunken, too, with sharp ridges about them, making the forehead forbiddingly narrow ; the upper lip, slightly lifted, shows the white teeth, rigidly clenched. The hair is heavy with moisture, the face as wet as the dewy grass all about. From his point of view the officer does not observe the rifle ; the man was apparently killed by the fall of the building.

"Dead a week," said the officer curtly, moving on and mechanically pulling out his watch as if to verify his estimate of time. Six o'clock and forty minutes.

Killed at Resaca

THE best soldier of our staff was Lieutenant Herman Brayle, one of the two aides-de-camp. I don't remember where the general picked him up ; from some Ohio regiment, I think ; none of us had previously known him, and it would have been strange if we had, for no two of us came from the same State, nor even from adjoining States. The general seemed to think that a position on his staff was a distinction that should be so judiciously conferred as not to beget any sectional jealousies and imperil the integrity of that part of the country which was still an integer. He would not even choose them from his own command, but by some jugglery at department headquarters obtained them from other brigades. Under such circumstances, a man's services had to be very distinguished indeed to be heard of by his family and the friends of his youth ; and "the speaking trump of fame" was a trifle hoarse from loquacity, anyhow.

Lieutenant Brayle was more than six feet in height and of splendid proportions, with the light hair and gray-blue eyes which men similarly gifted usually find associated with a high order of courage. As he was commonly in full uniform, especially in action, when most officers are content to be less flamboyantly attired, he was a very striking and conspicuous figure. As for the rest, he had a gentleman's manners, a scholar's head, and a lion's heart. His age was about thirty.

We all soon came to like Brayle as much as we admired him, and it was with sincere concern that in the engagement at Stone's River—our first action after he joined us— we observed that he had one most objectionable and unsoldierly quality : he was vain of his courage. During all the vicissitudes and mutations of that hideous encounter, whether our troops were fighting in the open cotton fields, in the cedar thickets, or behind the railway embankment, he did not once take cover, except when sternly commanded to do

so by the general, who commonly had other
things to think of than the lives of his staff
officers—or those of his men, for that matter.

In every later engagement while Brayle
was with us it was the same way. He
would sit his horse like an equestrian statue,
in a storm of bullets and grape, in the most
exposed places—wherever, in fact, duty, requiring him to go, permitted him to remain
—when, without trouble and with distinct
advantage to his reputation for common
sense, he might have been in such security
as is possible on a battle-field in the brief
intervals of personal inaction.

On foot, from necessity or in deference to
his dismounted commander or associates, his
conduct was the same. He would stand like
a rock in the open when officers and men
alike had taken to cover ; while men older
in service and years, higher in rank and of
unquestionable intrepidity, were loyally pre-
serving behind the crest of a hill lives in-
finitely precious to their country, this fellow
would stand, equally idle, on the ridge, facing in the direction of the sharpest fire.

When battles are going on in open ground
it frequently occurs that the opposing lines,

confronting each other within a stone's throw for hours, hug the earth as closely as if they loved it. The line officers in their proper places flatten themselves no less, and the field officers, their horses all killed or sent to the rear, crouch beneath the infernal canopy of hissing lead and screaming iron without a thought of personal dignity.

In such circumstances, the life of a staff officer of a brigade is distinctly "not a happy one," mainly because of its precarious tenure and the unnerving alternations of emotion to which he is exposed. From a position of that comparative security from which a civilian would ascribe his escape to a "miracle," he may be despatched with an order to some commander of a prone regiment in the front line—a person for the moment inconspicuous and not always easy to find without a deal of search among men somewhat preoccupied, and in a din in which question and answer alike must be imparted in the sign language. It is customary in such cases to duck the head and scuttle away on a keen run, an object of lively interest to some thousands of admiring marksmen. In returning—well it is not customary to return.

Brayle's practice was different. He would consign his horse to the care of an orderly,— he loved his horse,—and walk quietly away on his horrible errand with never a stoop of the back, his splendid figure, accentuated by his uniform, holding the eye with a strange fascination. We watched him with suspended breath, our hearts in our mouths. On one occasion of this kind, indeed, one of our number, an impetuous stammerer, was so possessed by his emotion that he shouted at me :

" I 'll b-b-bet you t-two d-d-dollars they d-drop him b-b-fore he g-gets to that d-d-ditch ! "

I did not accept the brutal wager ; I thought they would.

Let me do justice to a brave man's memory ; in all these needless exposures of life there was no visible bravado nor subsequent narration. In the few instances when some of us had ventured to remonstrate, Brayle had smiled pleasantly and made some light reply, which, however, had not encouraged a further pursuit of the subject. Once he said :—

" Captain, if ever I come to grief by forgetting your advice, I hope my last moments will be cheered by the sound of your beloved voice breathing into my ear the blessed words, ' I told you so.' ''

We laughed at the captain—just why we could probably not have explained—and that afternoon when he was shot to rags from an ambuscade Brayle remained by the body for some time, adjusting the limbs with needless care—there in the middle of a road swept by gusts of grape and canister ! It is easy to condemn this kind of thing, and not very difficult to refrain from imitation, but it is impossible not to respect, and Brayle was liked none the less for the weakness which had so heroic an expression. We wished he were not a fool, but he went on that way to the end, sometimes hard hit, but always returning to duty about as good as new.

Of course, it came at last ; he who ignores the law of probabilities challenges an adversary that is never beaten. It was at Resaca, in Georgia, during the movement that resulted in the capture of Atlanta. In front of our brigade the enemy's line of earthworks ran through open fields along a slight crest. At each end of this open ground we were close up to them in the woods, but the clear ground we could not hope to occupy until night, when the darkness would enable us to burrow like moles and throw up earth. At this point our line was a quarter-mile away in the edge of a wood. Roughly, we formed a semicircle, the enemy's fortified line being the chord of the arc.

"Lieutenant, go tell Colonel Ward to work up as close as he can get cover, and not to waste much ammunition in unnecessary firing. You may leave your horse."

When the general gave this direction we were in the fringe of the forest, near the right extremity of the arc. Colonel Ward was at the left. The suggestion to leave the horse obviously enough meant that Brayle was to take the longer line, through the woods and among the men. Indeed, the suggestion was needless ; to go by the short route meant absolutely certain failure to deliver the message. Before anybody could interpose, Brayle had cantered lightly into the field and the enemy's works were in crackling conflagration.

"Stop that damned fool !" shouted the general.

A private of the escort, with more ambition than brains, spurred forward to obey,
and within ten yards left himself and his
horse dead on the field of honor.

Brayle was beyond recall, galloping easily
along, parallel to the enemy and less than
two hundred yards distant. He was a picture to see ! His hat had been blown or
shot from his head, and his long, blond hair
rose and fell with the motion of his horse.
He sat erect in the saddle, holding the reins
lightly in his left hand, his right hanging
carelessly at his side. An occasional glimpse
of his handsome profile as he turned his
head one way or the other proved that the
interest which he took in what was going on
was natural and without affectation.

The picture was intensely dramatic, but in
no degree theatrical. Successive scores of
rifles spat at him viciously as he came within range, and our own line in the edge of the
timber broke out in visible and audible defense. No longer regardful of themselves or
their orders, our fellows sprang to their feet,
and, swarming into the open, sent broad
sheets of bullets against the blazing crest
of the offending works, which poured an

answering fire into their unprotected groups
with deadly effect. The artillery on both
sides joined the battle, punctuating the
rattle and roar with deep earth-shaking explosions and tearing the air with storms of
screaming grape, which, from the enemy's
side, splintered the trees and spattered them
with blood, and from ours defiled the smoke
of his arms with banks and clouds of dust
from his parapet.

My attention had been for a moment
averted to the general combat, but now,
glancing down the unobscured avenue between these two thunderclouds, I saw
Brayle, the cause of the carnage. Invisible
now from either side, and equally doomed
by friend and foe, he stood in the shot-swept
space, motionless, his face toward the enemy.
At some little distance lay his horse. I
instantly divined the cause of his inaction.

As topographical engineer I had, early in
the day, made a hasty examination of the
ground, and now remembered that at that
point was a deep and sinuous gully, crossing half the field from the enemy's line, its
general course at right angles to it. From
where we now were it was invisible, and

Brayle had evidently not known about it. Clearly, it was impassable. Its salient angles would have afforded him absolute security if he had chosen to be satisfied with the miracle already wrought in his favor and leap into it. He could not go forward, he would not turn back ; he stood awaiting death. It did not keep him long waiting.

By some mysterious coincidence, almost instantaneously as he fell, the firing ceased, a few desultory shots at long intervals serving rather to accentuate than break the silence. It was as if both sides had suddenly repented of their profitless crime. Four stretcher-bearers of ours, following a sergeant with a white flag, soon afterward moved unmolested into the field, and made straight for Brayle's body. Several Confederate officers and men came out to meet them, and, with uncovered heads, assisted them to take up their sacred burden. As it was borne away toward us we heard beyond the hostile works fifes and a muffled drum—a dirge. A generous enemy honored the fallen brave.

Amongst the dead man's effects was a soiled Russia-leather pocketbook. In the

7

distribution of mementoes of our friend, which the general, as administrator, decreed, this fell to me.

A year after the close of the war, on my way to California, I opened and idly inspected it. Out of an overlooked compartment fell a letter without envelope or address. It was in a woman's handwriting, and began with words of endearment, but no name.

It had the following date line : "San Francisco, Cal., July 9, 1862." The signature was " Darling," in marks of quotation. Incidentally, in the body of the text, the writer's full name was given — Marian Mendenhall.

The letter showed evidence of cultivation and good breeding, but it was an ordinary love letter, if a love letter can be ordinary. There was not much in it, but there was something. It was this :—

" Mr. Winters, whom I shall always hate for it, has been telling that at some battle in Virginia, where he got his hurt, you were seen crouching behind a tree. I think he wants to injure you in my regard, which he knows the story would do if I believed it.

I could bear to hear of my soldier lover's death, but not of his cowardice."

These were the words which on that sunny afternoon, in a distant region, had slain a hundred men. Is woman weak?

One evening I called on Miss Mendenhall to return the letter to her. I intended, also, to tell her what she had done—but not that she did it. I found her in a handsome dwelling on Rincon Hill. She was beautiful, well bred—in a word, charming.

" You knew Lieutenant Herman Brayle," I said, rather abruptly. " You know, doubtless, that he fell in battle. Among his effects was found this letter from you. My errand here is to place it in your hands."

She mechanically took the letter, glanced through it with deepening color, and then, looking at me with a smile, said :—

" It is very good of you, though I am sure it was hardly worth while." She started suddenly, and changed color. "This stain," she said, " is it—surely it is not——"

" Madam," I said, " pardon me, but that is the blood of the truest and bravest heart that ever beat."

She hastily flung the letter on the blazing

coals. "Uh! I cannot bear the sight of blood!" she said. "How did he die?"

I had involuntarily risen to rescue that scrap of paper, sacred even to me, and now stood partly behind her. As she asked the question she turned her face about and slightly upward. The light of the burning letter was reflected in her eyes, and touched her cheek with a tinge of crimson like the stain upon its page. I had never seen anything so beautiful as this detestable creature.

"He was bitten by a snake," I replied.

The Affair at Coulter's Notch

"DO you think, Colonel, that your brave Coulter would like to put one of his guns in here?" the general asked.

He was apparently not altogether serious; it certainly did not seem a place where any artillerist, however brave, would like to put a gun. The colonel thought that possibly his division commander meant good-humoredly to intimate that Captain Coulter's courage had been too highly extolled in a recent conversation between them.

"General," he replied warmly, "Coulter would like to put a gun anywhere within reach of those people," with a motion of his hand in the direction of the enemy.

"It is the only place," said the general. He was serious, then.

The place was a depression, a "notch,"

in the sharp crest of a hill. It was a pass,
and through it ran a turnpike, which, reaching this highest point in its course by a
sinuous ascent through a thin forest, made
a similar, though less steep, descent toward
the enemy. For a mile to the left and a mile
to the right, the ridge, though occupied by
Federal infantry lying close behind the sharp
crest and appearing as if held in place by
atmospheric pressure, was inaccessible to artillery. There was no place but the bottom
of the notch, and that was barely wide
enough for the roadbed. From the Confederate side this point was commanded by two
batteries posted on a slightly lower elevation
beyond a creek, and a half-mile away. All
the guns but one were masked by the trees
of an orchard ; that one—it seemed a bit of
impudence—was in an open lawn directly in
front of a rather grandiose building, the
planter's dwelling. The gun was safe enough
in its exposure—but only because the Federal
infantry had been forbidden to fire. Coulter's Notch—it came to be called so—was
not, that pleasant summer afternoon, a place
where one would ''like to put a gun.''

Three or four dead horses lay there,

sprawling in the road, three or four dead men in a trim row at one side of it, and a little back, down the hill. All but one were cavalrymen belonging to the Federal advance. One was a quartermaster. The general commanding the division, and the colonel commanding the brigade, with their staffs and escorts, had ridden into the notch to have a look at the enemy's guns—which had straightway obscured themselves in towering clouds of smoke. It was hardly profitable to be curious about guns which had the trick of the cuttlefish, and the season of observation was brief. At its conclusion—a short remove backward from where it began—occurred the conversation already partly reported. " It is the only place," the general repeated thoughtfully, "to get at them."

The colonel looked at him gravely. " There is room for but one gun, General— one against twelve."

" That is true—for only one at a time," said the commander with something like, yet not altogether like, a smile. " But then, your brave Coulter—a whole battery in himself."

The tone of irony was now unmistakable. It angered the colonel, but he did not know what to say. The spirit of military subordination is not favorable to retort, nor even deprecation. At this moment a young officer of artillery came riding slowly up the road attended by his bugler. It was Captain Coulter. He could not have been more than twenty-three years of age. He was of medium height, but very slender and lithe, and sat his horse with something of the air of a civilian. In face he was of a type singularly unlike the men about him ; thin, high-nosed, gray-eyed, with a slight blond mustache, and long, rather straggling hair of the same color. There was an apparent negligence in his attire. His cap was worn with the visor a trifle askew ; his coat was buttoned only at the sword-belt, showing a considerable expanse of white shirt, tolerably clean for that stage of the campaign. But the negligence was all in his dress and bearing ; in his face was a look of intense interest in his surroundings. His gray eyes, which seemed occasionally to strike right and left across the landscape, like search-lights, were for the most part fixed upon the sky beyond the Notch ; until he should arrive at the summit of the road there was nothing else in that direction to see. As he came opposite his division and brigade commanders at the roadside he saluted mechanically and was about to pass on. The colonel signed to him to halt.

"Captain Coulter," he said, "the enemy has twelve pieces over there on the next ridge. If I rightly understand the general, he directs that you bring up a gun and engage them."

There was a blank silence ; the general looked stolidly at a distant regiment swarming slowly up the hill through rough undergrowth, like a torn and draggled cloud of blue smoke ; the captain appeared not to have observed him. Presently the captain spoke, slowly and with apparent effort :

"On the next ridge, did you say, sir ? Are the guns near the house ? "

" Ah, you have been over this road before. Directly at the house."

" And it is—necessary—to engage them ? The order is imperative ? "

His voice was husky and broken. He was visibly paler. The colonel was astonished and mortified. He stole a glance at the commander. In that set, immobile face was no sign ; it was as hard as bronze. A moment later the general rode away, followed by his staff and escort. The colonel, humiliated and indignant, was about to order Captain Coulter in arrest, when the latter spoke a few words in a low tone to his bugler, saluted, and rode straight forward into the Notch, where, presently, at the summit of the road, his field glass at his eyes, he showed against the sky, he and his horse, sharply defined and motionless as an equestrian statue. The bugler had dashed down the road in the opposite direction at headlong speed and disappeared behind a wood. Presently his bugle was heard singing in the cedars, and in an incredibly short time a single gun with its caisson, each drawn by six horses and manned by its full complement of gunners, came bounding and banging up the grade in a storm of dust, unlimbered under cover, and was run forward by hand to the fatal crest among the dead horses. A gesture of the captain's arm, some strangely agile movements of the men in loading, and almost before the troops along the way had ceased to hear the rattle of the wheels, a great white cloud sprang forward down the slope, and with a deafening report the affair at Coulter's Notch had begun.

It is not intended to relate in detail the progress and incidents of that ghastly contest—a contest without vicissitudes, its alternations only different degrees of despair. Almost at the instant when Captain Coulter's gun blew its challenging cloud twelve answering clouds rolled upward from among the trees about the plantation house, a deep multiple report roared back like a broken echo, and thenceforth to the end the Federal cannoneers fought their hopeless battle in an atmosphere of living iron whose thoughts were lightnings and whose deeds were death.

Unwilling to see the efforts which he could not aid and the slaughter which he could not stay, the colonel ascended the ridge at a point a quarter of a mile to the left, whence the Notch, itself invisible, but pushing up successive masses of smoke, seemed the crater of a volcano in thundering eruption. With his glass he watched the

enemy's guns, noting as he could the effects
of Coulter's fire—if Coulter still lived to direct it.   He saw that the Federal gunners,
ignoring those of the enemy's pieces whose
positions could be determined by their smoke
only, gave their whole attention to the one
that maintained its place in the open—the
lawn in front of the house.   Over and about
that hardy piece the shells exploded at intervals of a few seconds.   Some exploded in
the house, as could be seen by thin ascen-
sions of smoke from the breached roof.   Figures of prostrate men and horses were plainly
visible.

" If our fellows are doing such good work
with a single gun," said the colonel to an
aide who happened to be nearest, " they
must be suffering like the devil from twelve.
Go down and present the commander of that
piece with my congratulations on the accu-
racy of his fire."

Turning to his adjutant-general he said,
" Did you observe Coulter's damned reluctance to obey orders ? "

" Yes, sir, I did."

" Well, say nothing about it, please.   I
don't think the general will care to make

any accusations. He will probably have enough to do in explaining his own connection with this uncommon way of amusing the rear-guard of a retreating enemy."

A young officer approached from below, climbing breathless up the acclivity. Almost before he had saluted, he gasped out:

"Colonel, I am directed by Colonel Harmon to say that the enemy's guns are within easy reach of our rifles, and most of them visible from various points along the ridge."

The brigade commander looked at him without a trace of interest in his expression. "I know it," he said quietly.

The young adjutant was visibly embarrassed. "Colonel Harmon would like to have permission to silence those guns," he stammered.

"So should I," the colonel said in the same tone. "Present my compliments to Colonel Harmon and say to him that the general's orders for the infantry not to fire are still in force."

The adjutant saluted and retired. The colonel ground his heel into the earth and turned to look again at the enemy's guns.

"Colonel," said the adjutant-general, "I don't know that I ought to say anything, but there is something wrong in all this. Do you happen to know that Captain Coulter is from the South?"

"No; *was* he, indeed?"

"I heard that last summer the division which the general then commanded was in the vicinity of Coulter's home—camped there for weeks, and——"

"Listen!" said the colonel, interrupting with an upward gesture. "Do you hear *that?*"

"That" was the silence of the Federal gun. The staff, the orderlies, the lines of infantry behind the crest—all had "heard," and were looking curiously in the direction of the crater, whence no smoke now ascended except desultory cloudlets from the enemy's shells. Then came the blare of a bugle, a faint rattle of wheels; a minute later the sharp reports recommenced with double activity. The demolished gun had been replaced with a sound one.

"Yes," said the adjutant-general, resuming his narrative, "the general made the acquaintance of Coulter's family. There was trouble—I don't know the exact nature of it—something about Coulter's wife. She is a red-hot Secessionist, as they all are, except Coulter himself, but she is a good wife and high-bred lady. There was a complaint to army headquarters. The general was transferred to this division. It is odd that Coulter's battery should afterward have been assigned to it."

The colonel had risen from the rock upon which they had been sitting. His eyes were blazing with a generous indignation.

"See here, Morrison," said he, looking his gossiping staff officer straight in the face, "did you get that story from a gentleman or a liar?"

"I don't want to say how I got it, Colonel, unless it is necessary "—he was blushing a trifle—"but I'll stake my life upon its truth in the main."

The colonel turned toward a small knot of officers some distance away. "Lieutenant Williams!" he shouted.

One of the officers detached himself from the group and coming forward saluted, saying: "Pardon me, Colonel, I thought you had been informed. Williams is dead

down there by the gun. What can I do,
sir?''

Lieutenant Williams was the aide who had
had the pleasure of conveying to the officer
in charge of the gun his brigade commander's congratulations.

"Go," said the colonel, "and direct the
withdrawal of that gun instantly. No—I 'll
go myself.''

He strode down the declivity toward the
rear of the Notch at a break-neck pace,
over rocks and through brambles, followed
by his little retinue in tumultuous disorder.
At the foot of the declivity they mounted
their waiting animals and took to the road
at a lively trot, round a bend and into the
Notch. The spectacle which they encountered there was appalling.

Within that defile, barely broad enough
for a single gun, were piled the wrecks of
no fewer than four. They had noted the
silencing of only the last one disabled—there
had been a lack of men to replace it quickly
with another. The débris lay on both sides
of the road ; the men had managed to keep
an open way between, through which the
fifth piece was now firing. The men ?—

they looked like demons of the pit! All were hatless, all stripped to the waist, their reeking skins black with blotches of powder and spattered with gouts of blood. They worked like madmen, with rammer and cartridge, lever and lanyard. They set their swollen shoulders and bleeding hands against the wheels at each recoil and heaved the heavy gun back to its place. There were no commands; in that awful environment of whooping shot, exploding shells, shrieking fragments of iron, and flying splinters of wood, none could have been heard. Officers, if officers there were, were indistinguishable; all worked together— each while he lasted—governed by the eye. When the gun was sponged, it was loaded; when loaded, aimed and fired. The colonel observed something new to his military experience—something horrible and unnatural: the gun was bleeding at the mouth! In temporary default of water, the man sponging had dipped his sponge in a pool of a comrade's blood. In all this work there was no clashing; the duty of the instant was obvious. When one fell, another, looking a trifle cleaner, seemed to rise from the earth in the dead man's tracks, to fall in his turn.

With the ruined guns lay the ruined men —alongside the wreckage, under it and atop of it; and back down the road—a ghastly procession!—crept on hands and knees such of the wounded as were able to move. The colonel—he had compassionately sent his cavalcade to the right about—had to ride over those who were entirely dead in order not to crush those who were partly alive. Into that hell he tranquilly held his way, rode up alongside the gun, and, in the obscurity of the last discharge, tapped upon the cheek the man holding the rammer—who straightway fell, thinking himself killed. A fiend seven times damned sprang out of the smoke to take his place, but paused and gazed up at the mounted officer with an unearthly regard, his teeth flashing between his black lips, his eyes, fierce and expanded, burning like coals beneath his bloody brow. The colonel made an authoritative gesture and pointed to the rear. The fiend bowed in token of obedience. It was Captain Coulter.

Simultaneously with the colonel's arrest-

ing sign, silence fell upon the whole field of
action.   The procession of missiles no longer
streamed into that defile of death, for the
enemy also had ceased firing. His army
had been gone for hours, and the commander
of his rear-guard, who had held his position
perilously long in hope to silence the Federal
fire, at that strange moment had silenced his
own.   " I was not aware of the breadth of
my authority," said the colonel to anybody,
riding forward to the crest to see what had
really happened.

An hour later his brigade was in bivouac
on the enemy's ground, and its idlers were
examining, with something of awe, as the
faithful inspect a saint's relics, a score of
straddling dead horses and three disabled
guns, all spiked. The fallen men had been
carried away ; their crushed and broken
bodies would have given too great satisfaction.

Naturally, the colonel established himself
and his military family in the plantation
house. It was somewhat shattered, but it
was better than the open air. The furniture
was greatly deranged and broken. The
walls and ceilings were knocked away here

and there, and a lingering odor of powder
smoke was everywhere. The beds, the
closets of women's clothing, the cupboards
were not greatly damaged. The new ten-
ants for a night made themselves comfortable, and the virtual effacement of Coulter's
battery supplied them with an interesting
topic.

During supper an orderly of the escort
showed himself into the dining-room and
asked permission to speak to the colonel.

"What is it, Barbour?" said that officer
pleasantly, having overheard the request.

"Colonel, there is something wrong in the
cellar; I don't know what—somebody there.
I was down there rummaging about."

"I will go down and see," said a staff
officer, rising.

"So will I," the colonel said; "let the
others remain. Lead on, orderly."

They took a candle from the table and de-
scended the cellar stairs, the orderly in visible trepidation. The candle made but a
feeble light, but presently, as they advanced,
its narrow circle of illumination revealed a
human figure seated on the ground against
the black stone wall which they were skirt-

ing, its knees elevated, its head bowed
sharply forward. The face, which should
have been seen in profile, was invisible, for
the man was bent so far forward that his
long hair concealed it ; and, strange to relate, the beard, of a much darker hue, fell in
a great tangled mass and lay along the
ground at his feet. They involuntarily
paused ; then the colonel, taking the candle
from the orderly's shaking hand, approached
the man and attentively considered him.
The long dark beard was the hair of a woman
—dead. The dead woman clasped in her
arms a dead babe. Both were clasped in
the arms of the man, pressed against his
breast, against his lips. There was blood in
the hair of the woman ; there was blood in
the hair of the man. A yard away, near
an irregular depression in the beaten earth
which formed the cellar's floor—a fresh excavation with a convex bit of iron, having
jagged edges, visible in one of the sides—lay
an infant's foot. The colonel held the light
as high as he could. The floor of the room
above was broken through, the splinters
pointing at all angles downward. "This
casemate is not bomb-proof," said the

colonel gravely. It did not occur to him that his summing up of the matter had any levity in it.

They stood about the group awhile in silence ; the staff officer was thinking of his unfinished supper, the orderly of what might possibly be in one of the casks on the other side of the cellar. Suddenly the man whom they had thought dead raised his head and gazed tranquilly into their faces. His complexion was coal black ; the cheeks were apparently tattooed in irregular sinuous lines from the eyes downward. The lips, too, were white, like those of a stage negro. There was blood upon his forehead.

The staff officer drew back a pace, the orderly two paces.

"What are you doing here, my man?" said the colonel, unmoved.

"This house belongs to me, sir," was the reply, civilly delivered.

"To you? Ah, I see ! And these?"

"My wife and child. I am Captain Coulter."

A Tough Tussle

ONE night in the autumn of 1861 a man
sat alone in the heart of a forest in
Western Virginia. The region was then,
and still is, one of the wildest on the conti-
nent—the Cheat Mountain country. There
was no lack of people close at hand, however ; within two miles of where the man
sat was the now silent camp of a whole
Federal brigade. Somewhere about—it
might be still nearer—was a force of the
enemy, the numbers unknown. It was this
uncertainty as to its numbers and position
that accounted for the man's presence in
that lonely spot ; he was a young officer of
a Federal infantry regiment, and his business
there was to guard his sleeping comrades in
the camp against a surprise. He was in command of a detachment of men constituting

a picket-guard. These men he had stationed
just at nightfall in an irregular line, determined by the nature of the ground, several
hundred yards in front of where he now sat.
The line ran through the forest, among the
rocks and laurel thickets, the men fifteen or
twenty paces apart, all in concealment and
under injunction of strict silence and unre-
mitting vigilance. In four hours, if nothing
occurred, they would be relieved by a fresh
detachment from the reserve now resting in
care of its captain some distance away to
the left and rear. Before stationing his men
the young officer of whom we are speaking
had pointed out to his two sergeants the spot
at which he would be found in case it should
be necessary to consult him, or if his presence
at the front line should be required.

It was a quiet enough spot—the fork of
an old wood-road, on the two branches of
which, prolonging themselves deviously forward in the dim moonlight, the sergeants
were themselves stationed, a few paces in
rear of the line. If driven sharply back by
a sudden onset of the enemy—and pickets
are not expected to make a stand after firing—the men would come into the converg-

ing roads, and, naturally following them to their point of intersection, could be rallied and "formed." In his small way the author of these dispositions was something of a strategist ; if Napoleon had planned as intelligently at Waterloo, he would have won the battle and been overthrown later.

Second Lieutenant Brainerd Byring was a brave and efficient officer, young and comparatively inexperienced as he was in the business of killing his fellow-men. He had enlisted in the very first days of the war as a private, with no military knowledge whatever, had been made first sergeant of his company on account of his education and engaging manner, and had been lucky enough to lose his captain by a Confederate bullet ; in the resulting promotions he had got a commission. He had been in several engagements, such as they were—at Philippi, Rich Mountain, Carrick's Ford and Greenbrier—and had borne himself with such gallantry as not to attract the attention of his superior officers. The exhilaration of battle was agreeable to him, but the sight of the dead, with their clay faces, blank eyes, and stiff bodies, which, when not unnaturally shrunken, were unnaturally swollen, had always intolerably affected him. He felt toward them a kind of reasonless antipathy which was something more than the physical and spiritual repugnance common to us all. Doubtless this feeling was due to his unusually acute sensibilities—his keen sense of the beautiful, which these hideous things outraged. Whatever may have been the cause, he could not look upon a dead body without a loathing which had in it an element of resentment. What others have respected as the dignity of death had to him no existence—was altogether unthinkable. Death was a thing to be hated. It was not picturesque, it had no tender and solemn side—a dismal thing, hideous in all its manifestations and suggestions. Lieutenant Byring was a braver man than anybody knew, for nobody knew his horror of that which he was ever ready to incur.

Having posted his men, instructed his sergeants, and retired to his station, he seated himself on a log, and with senses all alert began his vigil. For greater ease he loosened his sword-belt, and, taking his heavy revolver from his holster, laid it on

the log beside him. He felt very comfortable, though he hardly gave the fact a
thought, so intently did he listen for any
sound from the front which might have a
menacing significance—a shout, a shot, or
the footfall of one of his sergeants coming to
apprise him of something worth knowing.
From the vast, invisible ocean of moonlight
overhead fell, here and there, a slender,
broken stream that seemed to plash against
the intercepting branches and trickle to
earth, forming small white pools among the
clumps of laurel. But these leaks were few
and served only to accentuate the blackness
of his environment, which his imagination
found it easy to people with all manner of
unfamiliar shapes, menacing, uncanny, or
merely grotesque.

He to whom the portentous conspiracy of
night and solitude and silence in the heart
of a great forest is not an unknown experience needs not to be told what another world
it all is—how even the most commonplace
and familiar objects take on another character. The trees group themselves differently ;
they draw closer together, as if in fear. The
very silence has another quality than the

silence of the day. And it is full of half-heard whispers, whispers that startle—ghosts of sounds long dead. There are living sounds, too, such as are never heard under other conditions : notes of strange night-birds, the cries of small animals in sudden encounters with stealthy foes, or in their dreams, a rustling in the dead leaves—it may be the leap of a wood-rat, it may be the footfall of a panther. What caused the breaking of that twig?—what the low, alarmed twittering in that bushful of birds ? There are sounds without a name, forms without substance, translations in space of objects which have not been seen to move, movements wherein nothing is observed to change its place. Ah, children of the sunlight and the gaslight, how little you know of the world in which you live !

Surrounded at a little distance by armed and watchful friends, Byring felt utterly alone. Yielding himself to the solemn and mysterious spirit of the time and place, he had forgotten the nature of his connection with the visible and audible aspects and phases of the night. The forest was boundless ; men and the habitations of men did

not exist. The universe was one primeval
mystery of darkness, without form and void,
himself the sole dumb questioner of its eternal secret. Absorbed in the thoughts born
of this mood, he suffered the time to slip
away unnoted. Meantime the infrequent
patches of white light lying amongst the
undergrowth had undergone changes of size,
form, and place. In one of them near by,
just at the roadside, his eye fell upon an
object which he had not previously observed.
It was almost before his face as he sat ; he
could have sworn that it had not before been
there. It was partly covered in shadow,
but he could see that it was a human figure.
Instinctively he adjusted the clasp of his
sword-belt and laid hold of his pistol—again
he was in a world of war, by occupation an
assassin.

The figure did not move. Rising, pistol
in hand, he approached. The figure lay
upon its back, its upper part in shadow, but
standing above it and looking down upon the
face, he saw that it was a dead body. He
shuddered and turned from it with a feeling
of sickness and disgust, resumed his seat
upon the log, and, forgetting military pru-

dence, struck a match and lit a cigar. In the sudden blackness that followed the extinction of the flame he felt a sense of relief ; he could no longer see the object of his aversion. Nevertheless, he kept his eyes set in that direction until it appeared again with growing distinctness. It seemed to have moved a trifle nearer.

"Damn the thing!" he muttered. "What does it want?"

It did not appear to be in need of anything but a soul.

Byring turned away his eyes and began humming a tune, but he broke off in the middle of a bar and looked at the dead body. Its presence annoyed him, though he could hardly have had a quieter neighbor. He was conscious, too, of a vague, indefinable feeling which was new to him. It was not fear, but rather a sense of the supernatural— in which he did not at all believe.

"I have inherited it," he said to himself. "I suppose it will require a thousand years— perhaps ten thousand—for humanity to outgrow this feeling. Where and when did it originate? Away back, probably, in what is called the cradle of the human race—the

plains of Central Asia. What we inherit as
a superstition our barbarous ancestors must
have held as a reasonable conviction. Doubtless they believed themselves justified by
facts whose nature we cannot even conjecture
in thinking a dead body a malign thing en-
dowed with some strange power of mischief,
with perhaps a will and a purpose to exert it.
Possibly they had some awful form of religion
of which that was one of the chief doctrines,
sedulously taught by their priesthood, just
as ours teach the immortality of the soul.
As the Aryan moved westward to and
through the Caucasus passes and spread
over Europe, new conditions of life must
have resulted in the formulation of new re-
ligions. The old belief in the malevolence
of the dead body was lost from the creeds,
and even perished from tradition, but it left
its heritage of terror, which is transmitted
from generation to generation—is as much
a part of us as our blood and bones."

In following out his thought he had forgotten that which suggested it ; but now his
eye fell again upon the corpse. The shadow
had now altogether uncovered it. He saw
the sharp profile, the chin in the air, the

whole face, ghastly white in the moonlight. The clothing was gray, the uniform of a Confederate soldier. The coat and waistcoat, unbuttoned, had fallen away on each side, exposing the white shirt. The chest seemed unnaturally prominent, but the abdomen had sunk in, leaving a sharp projection at the line of the lower ribs. The arms were extended, the left knee was thrust upward. The whole posture impressed Byring as having been studied with a view to the horrible.

" Bah ! " he exclaimed ; " he was an actor—he knows how to be dead."

He drew away his eyes, directing them resolutely along one of the roads leading to the front, and resumed his philosophizing where he had left off.

" It may be that our Central Asian ancestors had not the custom of burial. In that case it is easy to understand their fear of the dead, who really were a menace and an evil. They bred pestilences. Children were taught to avoid the places where they lay, and to run away if by inadvertence they came near a corpse. I think, indeed, I 'd better go away from this chap."

He half rose to do so, then remembered that he had told his men in front, and the officer in the rear who was to relieve him, that he could at any time be found at that spot. It was a matter of pride, too. If he abandoned his post, he feared they would think he feared the corpse. He was no coward, and he was unwilling to incur anybody's ridicule. So he again seated himself, and to prove his courage looked boldly at the body. The right arm—the one farthest from him—was now in shadow. He could barely see the hand which, he had before observed, lay at the root of a clump of laurel. There had been no change, a fact which gave him a certain comfort, he could not have said why. He did not at once remove his eyes; that which we do not wish to see has a strange fascination, sometimes irresistible. Of the woman who covers her eyes with her hands and looks between the fingers, let it be said that the wits have dealt with her not altogether justly.

Byring suddenly became conscious of a pain in his right hand. He withdrew his eyes from his enemy and looked at it. He was grasping the hilt of his drawn sword so tightly that it hurt him. He observed, too, that he was leaning forward in a strained attitude—crouching like a gladiator ready to spring at the throat of an antagonist. His teeth were clenched, and he was breathing hard. This matter was soon set right, and as his muscles relaxed and he drew a long breath, he felt keenly enough the ludicrousness of the incident. It affected him to laughter. Heavens ! what sound was that? what mindless devil was uttering an unholy glee in mockery of human merriment ? He sprang to his feet and looked about him, not recognizing his own laugh.

He could no longer conceal from himself the horrible fact of his cowardice ; he was thoroughly frightened ! He would have run from the spot, but his legs refused their office ; they gave way beneath him, and he sat again upon the log, violently trembling. His face was wet, his whole body bathed in a chill perspiration. He could not even cry out. Distinctly he heard behind him a stealthy tread, as of some wild animal, and dared not look over his shoulder. Had the soulless living joined forces with the soulless dead ?—was it an animal? Ah, if he could

but be assured of that ! But by no effort of
will could he now unfix his gaze from the
face of the dead man.

I repeat that Lieutenant Byring was a
brave and intelligent man. But what would
you have? Shall a man cope, single-handed,
with so monstrous an alliance as that of night
and solitude and silence and the dead?—
while an incalculable host of his own ancestors shriek into the ear of his spirit their
coward counsel, sing their doleful death-
songs in his heart, and disarm his very blood
of all its iron? The odds are too great—
courage was not made for such rough use as
that.

One sole conviction now had the man in
possession : that the body had moved. It
lay nearer to the edge of its plot of light—
there could be no doubt of it. It had also
moved its arms, for, look, they are both in
the shadow ! A breath of cold air struck
Byring full in the face ; the branches of trees
above him stirred and moaned. A strongly
defined shadow passed across the face of the
dead, left it luminous, passed back upon it,
and left it half obscured. The horrible thing
was visibly moving ! At that moment a

single shot rang out upon the picket-line—a
lonelier and louder, though more distant,
shot than ever had been heard by mortal
ear ! It broke the spell of that enchanted
man ; it slew the silence and the solitude,
dispersed the hindering host from Central
Asia, and released his modern manhood.
With a cry like that of some great bird
pouncing upon its prey, he sprang forward,
hot-hearted for action !

Shot after shot now came from the front.
There were shoutings and confusion, hoof-
beats and desultory cheers. Away to the
rear, in the sleeping camp, were a singing
of bugles and grumble of drums. Pushing
through the thickets on either side the roads
came the Federal pickets, in full retreat, firing backward at random as they ran. A
straggling group that had followed back one
of the roads, as instructed, suddenly sprang
away into the bushes as half a hundred
horsemen thundered by them, striking
wildly with their sabres as they passed. At
headlong speed these mounted madmen shot
past the spot where Byring had sat, and
vanished round an angle of the road, shouting and firing their pistols. A moment later

there was a roar of musketry, followed by dropping shots—they had encountered the reserve-guard in line ; and back they came in dire confusion, with here and there an empty saddle and many a maddened horse, bullet-stung, snorting and plunging with pain. It was all over—"an affair of outposts."

The line was re-established with fresh men, the roll called, the stragglers were re-formed. The Federal commander, with a part of his staff, imperfectly clad, appeared upon the scene, asked a few questions, looked exceedingly wise, and retired. After standing at arms for an hour, the brigade in camp "swore a prayer or two " and went to bed.

Early the next morning a fatigue-party, commanded by a captain and accompanied by a surgeon, searched the ground for dead and wounded. At the fork af the road, a little to one side, they found two bodies lying close together—that of a Federal officer and that of a Confederate private. The officer had died of a sword-thrust through the heart, but not, apparently, until he had inflicted upon his enemy no fewer than five dreadful wounds. The dead officer lay on his face in a pool of blood, the weapon still in his breast. They turned him on his back and the surgeon removed it.

" Gad ! " said the captain—" it is By-ring ! "—adding, with a glance at the other, " They had a tough tussle."

The surgeon was examining the sword. It was that of a line officer of Federal in-fantry—exactly like the one worn by the captain. It was, in fact, Byring's own. The only other weapon discovered was an undischarged revolver in the dead officer's belt.

The surgeon laid down the sword and ap-proached the other body. It was frightfully gashed and stabbed, but there was no blood. He took hold of the left foot and tried to straighten the leg. In the effort the body was displaced. The dead do not wish to be moved—it protested with a faint, sickening odor. Where it had lain were a few mag-gots, manifesting an imbecile activity.

The surgeon looked at the captain. The captain looked at the surgeon.

The Coup de Grâce

THE fighting had been hard and continuous, that was attested by all the senses. The very taste of battle was in the air. All was now over; it remained only to succor the wounded and bury the dead—to "tidy up a bit," as the humorist of a burial squad put it. A good deal of "tidying up" was required. As far as one could see through the forest, between the splintered trees, lay wrecks of men and horses. Among them moved the stretcher-bearers, gathering and carrying away the few who showed signs of life. Most of the wounded had died of neglect while the right to minister to their wants was in dispute. It is an army regulation that the wounded must wait; the best way to care for them is to win the battle. It must be confessed that victory is a dis-

tinct advantage to a man requiring attention,
but many do not live to avail themselves of
it.

The dead were collected in groups of a
dozen or a score and laid side by side in
rows while the trenches were dug to receive
them. Some, found at too great a distance
from these rallying points, were buried
where they lay. There was little attempt
at identification, though in most cases, the
buryial parties being detailed to glean the
same ground which they had assisted to
reap, the names of the victorious dead were
known and listed. The enemy's fallen had
to be content with counting. But of that
they got enough : many of them were
counted several times, and the total, as
given afterward in the official report of the
victorious commander, denoted rather a
hope than a result.

At some little distance from the spot
where one of the burial parties had established its "bivouac of the dead," a man in
the uniform of a Federal officer stood leaning against a tree. From his feet upward
to his neck his attitude was that of weariness reposing ; but he turned his head un-

easily from side to side; his mind was apparently not at rest. He was perhaps uncertain in what direction to go; he was not likely to remain long where he was, for already the level rays of the setting sun struggled redly through the open spaces of the wood, and the weary soldiers were quitting their task for the day. He would hardly make a night of it alone there among the dead. Nine men in ten whom you meet after a battle inquire the way to some fraction of the army—as if anyone could know. Doubtless this officer was lost. After resting himself a moment, he would follow one of the retiring burial squads.

When all were gone, he walked straight away into the forest toward the red west, its light staining his face like blood. The air of confidence with which he now strode along showed that he was on familiar ground; he had recovered his bearings. The dead on his right and on his left were unregarded as he passed. An occasional low moan from some sorely-stricken wretch whom the relief-parties had not reached, and who would have to pass a comfortless night beneath the stars with his thirst to keep him company, was equally unheeded. What, indeed, could the officer have done, being no surgeon and having no water?

At the head of a shallow ravine, a mere depression of the ground, lay a small group of bodies. He saw, and, swerving suddenly from his course, walked rapidly toward them. Scanning each one sharply as he passed, he stopped at last above one which lay at a slight remove from the others, near a clump of small trees. He looked at it narrowly. It seemed to stir. He stooped and laid his hand upon its face. It screamed.

The officer was Captain Downing Madwell, of a Massachusetts regiment of infantry, a daring and intelligent soldier, an honorable man.

In the regiment were two brothers named Halcrow—Caffal and Creede Halcrow. Caffal Halcrow was a sergeant in Captain Madwell's company, and these two men, the sergeant and the captain, were devoted friends. In so far as disparity of rank, difference in duties, and considerations of military discipline would permit, they were commonly together. They had, indeed, grown up together from childhood. A habit of the heart is not easily broken off. Caffal Halcrow had nothing military in his taste or disposition, but the thought of separation from his friend was disagreeable ; he enlisted in the company in which Madwell was second lieutenant. Each had taken two steps upward in rank, but between the highest non-commissioned and the lowest commissioned officer the gulf is deep and wide and the old relation was maintained with difficulty and a difference.

Creede Halcrow, the brother of Caffal, was the major of the regiment—a cynical, saturnine man, between whom and Captain Madwell there was a natural antipathy which circumstances had nourished and strengthened to an active animosity. But for the restraining influence of their mutual relation to Caffal these two patriots would doubtless have endeavored to deprive their country of each other's services.

At the opening of the battle that morning, the regiment was performing outpost duty a mile away from the main army. It was attacked and nearly surrounded in the forest, but stubbornly held its ground. During a lull in the fighting, Major Halcrow came to Captain Madwell. The two exchanged formal salutes, and the major said : " Captain, the colonel directs that you push your company to the head of this ravine and hold your place there until recalled. I need hardly apprise you of the dangerous character of the movement, but if you wish, you can, I suppose, turn over the command to your first lieutenant. I was not, however, directed to authorize the substitution ; it is merely a suggestion of my own, unofficially made."

To this deadly insult Captain Madwell coolly replied :—

"Sir, I invite you to accompany the movement. A mounted officer would be a conspicuous mark, and I have long held the opinion that it would be better if you were dead."

The art of repartee was cultivated in military circles as early as 1862.

A half-hour later Captain Madwell's company was driven from its position at the head of the ravine, with a loss of one third its number. Among the fallen was Sergeant Halcrow. The regiment was soon afterward forced back to the main line, and at the close of the battle was miles away. The captain was now standing at the side of his subordinate and friend.

Sergeant Halcrow was mortally hurt. His clothing was deranged ; it seemed to have been violently torn apart, exposing the abdomen. Some of the buttons of his jacket had been pulled off and lay on the ground beside him, and fragments of his other garments were strewn about. His leather belt was parted, and had apparently been dragged from beneath him as he lay. There had been no great effusion of blood. The only visible wound was a wide, ragged opening in the abdomen. It was defiled with earth and dead leaves. Protruding from it was a loop of small intestine. In all his experience Captain Madwell had not seen a wound like this. He could neither conjecture how it was made, nor explain the attendant circumstances—the strangely torn clothing, the parted belt, the besmirching of the white skin. He knelt and made a closer examination. When he rose to his feet, he turned his eyes in various directions as if looking for an enemy. Fifty yards away, on the

crest of a low, thinly wooded hill, he saw
several dark objects moving about among
the fallen men—a herd of swine. One
stood with its back to him, its shoulders
sharply elevated. Its forefeet were upon a
human body, its head was depressed and
invisible. The bristly ridge of its chine
showed black against the red west. Captain
Madwell drew away his eyes and fixed them
again upon the thing which had been his
friend.

The man who had suffered these monstrous mutilations was alive. At intervals
he moved his limbs; he moaned at every
breath. He stared blankly into the face of
his friend, and if touched screamed. In his
giant agony he had torn up the ground on
which he lay ; his clenched hands were full
of leaves and twigs and earth. Articulate
speech was beyond his power ; it was impossible to know if he were sensible to anything but pain. The expression of his face
was an appeal ; his eyes were full of prayer.
For what ?

There was no misreading that look ; the
captain had too frequently seen it in eyes of
those whose lips had still the power to

formulate it by an entreaty for death. Consciously or unconsciously, this writhing fragment of humanity, this type and example of acute sensation, this handiwork of man and beast, this humble, unheroic Prometheus, was imploring everything, all, the whole non-*ego*, for the boon of oblivion. To the earth and the sky alike, to the trees, to the man, to whatever took form in sense or consciousness, this incarnate suffering addressed his silent plea.

For what, indeed? For that we accord to even the meanest creature without sense to demand it, denying it only to the wretched of our own race: for the blessed release, the rite of uttermost compassion, the *coup de grâce*.

Captain Madwell spoke the name of his friend. He repeated it over and over without effect until emotion choked his utterance. His tears plashed upon the livid face beneath his own and blinded himself. He saw nothing but a blurred and moving object, but the moans were more distinct than ever, interrupted at briefer intervals by sharper shrieks. He turned away, struck his hand upon his forehead, and strode from the spot. The swine, catching sight of him, threw up their crimson muzzles, regarding him suspiciously a second, and then, with a gruff, concerted grunt, raced away out of sight. A horse, its foreleg splintered horribly by a cannon-shot, lifted its head sidewise from the ground and neighed piteously. Madwell stepped forward, drew his revolver, and shot the poor beast between the eyes, narrowly observing its death-struggle, which, contrary to his expectation, was violent and long ; but at last it lay still. The tense muscles of its lips, which had uncovered the teeth in a horrible grin, relaxed ; the sharp, clean-cut profile took on a look of profound peace and rest.

Along the distant thinly wooded crest to westward the fringe of sunset fire had now nearly burned itself out. The light upon the trunks of the trees had faded to a tender gray ; shadows were in their tops, like great dark birds aperch. Night was coming and there were miles of haunted forest between Captain Madwell and camp. Yet he stood there at the side of the dead animal, apparently lost to all sense of his surroundings. His eyes were bent upon the earth at his feet ; his left hand hung loosely at his side, his right still held the pistol. Suddenly he lifted his face, turned it toward his dying friend, and walked rapidly back to his side. He knelt upon one knee, cocked the weapon, placed the muzzle against the man's forehead, and turning away his eyes, pulled the trigger. There was no report. He had used his last cartridge for the horse.

The sufferer moaned and his lips moved convulsively. The froth that ran from them had a tinge of blood.

Captain Madwell rose to his feet and drew his sword from the scabbard. He passed the fingers of his left hand along the edge from hilt to point. He held it out straight before him, as if to test his nerves. There was no visible tremor of the blade ; the ray of bleak skylight that it reflected was steady and true. He stooped, and with his left hand tore away the dying man's shirt, rose, and placed the point of the sword just over the heart. This time he did not withdraw his eyes. Grasping the hilt with both hands, he thrust downward with all his strength and weight. The blade sank into the man's body—through his body into the

earth ; Captain Madwell came near falling
forward upon his work. The dying man
drew up his knees and at the same time
threw his right arm across his breast and
grasped the steel so tightly that the knuck-
les of the hand visibly whitened. By a
violent but vain effort to withdraw the
blade, the wound was enlarged ; a rill of
blood escaped, running sinuously down into
the deranged clothing. At that moment
three men stepped silently forward from behind the clump of young trees which had
concealed their approach. Two were hos-
pital attendants and carried a stretcher.

The third was Major Creede Halcrow.

Parker Adderson, Philosopher

"PRISONER, what is your name?"

"As I am to lose it at daylight to-morrow morning, it is hardly worth concealing. Parker Adderson."

"Your rank?"

"A somewhat humble one; commissioned officers are too precious to be risked in the perilous business of a spy. I am a sergeant."

"Of what regiment?"

"You must excuse me; my answer might, for anything I know, give you an idea of whose forces are in your front. Such knowledge as that is what I came into your lines to obtain, not to impart."

"You are not without wit."

"If you have the patience to wait, you will find me dull enough to-morrow."

"How do you know that you are to die to-morrow morning?"

"Among spies captured by night that is the custom. It is one of the nice observances of the profession."

The general so far laid aside the dignity appropriate to a Confederate officer of high rank and wide renown as to smile. But no one in his power and out of his favor would have drawn any happy augury from that outward and visible sign of approval. It was neither genial nor infectious ; it did not communicate itself to the other persons exposed to it—the caught spy who had provoked it and the armed guard who had brought him into the tent and now stood a little apart, watching his prisoner in the yellow candle-light. It was no part of that warrior's duty to smile ; he had been detailed for another purpose. The conversation was resumed ; it was, in character, a trial for a capital offense.

"You admit, then, that you are a spy— that you came into my camp, disguised as you are in the uniform of a Confederate soldier, to obtain information secretly regarding the numbers and disposition of my troops."

"Regarding, particularly, their numbers. Their disposition I already knew. It is morose."

The general brightened again ; the guard, with a severer sense of his responsibility, accentuated the austerity of his expression and stood a trifle more erect than before. Twirling his gray slouch hat round and round upon his forefinger, the spy took a leisurely survey of his surroundings. They were simple enough. The tent was a common "wall tent," about eight feet by ten in dimensions, lighted by a single tallow candle stuck into the haft of a bayonet, which was itself stuck into a pine table, at which the general sat, now busily writing and apparently forgetful of his unwilling guest. An old rag carpet covered the earthen floor ; an older hair trunk, a second chair, and a roll of blankets were about all else that the tent contained ; in General Clavering's command Confederate simplicity and penury of "pomp and circumstance" had attained their highest development. On a large nail driven into the tent pole at the entrance was suspended a sword-belt supporting a long sabre, a pistol in its holster, and, absurdly enough, a bowie knife. Of that most unmilitary weapon it was the general's habit to explain that it was a cherished souvenir of the peaceful days when he was a civilian.

It was a stormy night. The rain cascaded upon the canvas in torrents, with the dull, drum-like sound familiar to dwellers in tents. As the whooping blasts charged upon it the frail structure shook and swayed and strained at its confining stakes and ropes.

The general finished writing, folded the half-sheet of paper, and spoke to the soldier guarding Adderson : "Here, Tassman, take that to the adjutant-general ; then return."

"And the prisoner, General?" said the soldier, saluting, with an inquiring glance in the direction of that unfortunate.

"Do as I said," replied the officer, curtly.

The soldier took the note and ducked himself out of the tent. General Clavering turned his handsome, clean-cut face toward the Federal spy, looked him in the eyes, not unkindly, and said : "It is a bad night, my man."

"For me, yes."

"Do you guess what I have written?"

"Something worth reading, I dare say. And—perhaps it is my vanity—I venture to suppose that I am mentioned in it."

"Yes ; it is a memorandum for an order to be read to the troops at *reveille* concerning your execution. Also some notes for the guidance of the provost-marshal in arranging the details of that event."

"I hope, General, the spectacle will be intelligently arranged, for I shall attend it myself."

"Have you any arrangements of your own that you wish to make ? Do you wish to see a chaplain, for example ?"

"I could hardly secure a longer rest for myself by depriving him of some of his."

"Good God, man ! do you mean to go to your death with nothing but jokes upon your lips ? Do you know that this is a serious matter ? "

"How can I know that ? I have never been dead in all my life. I have heard that death is a serious matter, but never from any of those who have experienced it."

The general was silent for a moment ; the man interested, perhaps amused him—a type not previously encountered.

"Death," he said, "is at least a loss—a loss of such happiness as we have, and of opportunities for more."

"A loss of which we will never be conscious can be borne with composure and therefore expected without apprehension. You must have observed, General, that of all the dead men with whom it is your soldierly pleasure to strew your path, none show signs of regret."

"If the being dead is not a regrettable condition, yet the becoming so—the act of dying—appears to be distinctly disagreeable in one who has not lost the power to feel."

"Pain is disagreeable, no doubt. I never suffer it without more or less discomfort. But he who lives longest is most exposed to it. What you call dying is simply the last pain—there is really no such thing as dying. Suppose, for illustration, that I attempt to escape. You lift the revolver that you are courteously concealing in your lap, and—"

The general blushed like a girl, then laughed softly, disclosing his brilliant teeth, made a slight inclination of his handsome head, and said nothing. The spy continued: "You fire, and I have in my stomach what I did not swallow. I fall, but am not dead. After a half-hour of agony I am dead. But at any given instant of that half-hour I was either alive or dead. There is no transition period.

"When I am hanged to-morrow morning it will be quite the same ; while conscious I shall be living ; when dead, unconscious. Nature appears to have ordered the matter quite in my interest—the way that I should have ordered it myself. It is so simple," he added with a smile, "that it seems hardly worth while to be hanged at all."

At the finish of his remarks there was a long silence. The general sat impassive, looking into the man's face, but apparently not attentive to what had been said. It was as if his eyes had mounted guard over the prisoner, while his mind concerned itself with other matters. Presently he drew a long, deep breath, shuddered, as one awakened from a dreadful dream, and exclaimed almost inaudibly : " Death is horrible ! "—this man of death.

" It was horrible to our savage ancestors," said the spy, gravely, " because they had not enough intelligence to dissociate the idea of consciousness from the idea of the physical forms in which it is manifested—as an even lower order of intelligence, that of the monkey, for example, may be unable to imagine a house without inhabitants, and seeing a ruined hut fancies a suffering occupant. To us it is horrible because we have inherited the tendency to think it so, accounting for the notion by wild and fanciful theories of another world—as names of places give rise to legends explaining them, and reasonless conduct to philosophies in justification. You can hang me, General, but there your power of evil ends; you cannot condemn me to heaven."

The general appeared not to have heard; the spy's talk had merely turned his thoughts into an unfamiliar channel, but there they pursued their will independently to conclusions of their own. The storm had ceased, and something of the solemn spirit of the night had imparted itself to his reflections, giving them the sombre tinge of a supernatural dread. Perhaps there was an element of prescience in it. "I should not like to die," he said—"not to-night."

He was interrupted—if, indeed, he had

intended to speak further—by the entrance of an officer of his staff, Captain Hasterlick, the provost-marshal. This recalled him to himself; the absent look passed away from his face.

"Captain," he said, acknowledging the officer's salute, "this man is a Yankee spy captured inside our lines with incriminating papers on him. He has confessed. How is the weather?"

"The storm is over, sir, and the moon shining."

"Good; take a file of men, conduct him at once to the parade ground, and shoot him."

A sharp cry broke from the spy's lips. He threw himself forward, thrust out his neck, expanded his eyes, clenched his hands.

"Good God!" he cried hoarsely, almost inarticulately; "you do not mean that! You forget—I am not to die until morning."

"I have said nothing of morning," replied the general, coldly; "that was an assumption of your own. You die now."

"But, General, I beg—I implore you to remember; I am to hang! It will take some

time to erect the gallows—two hours—an
hour.   Spies are hanged ; I have rights
under military law.   For heaven's sake,
General, consider how short—"

" Captain, observe my directions."

The officer drew his sword, and, fixing his
eyes upon the prisoner, pointed silently to the
opening of the tent.   The prisoner, deathly
pale, hesitated ; the officer grasped him by
the collar and pushed him gently forward.
As he approached the tent pole, the frantic
man sprang to it, and, with cat-like agility,
seized the handle of the bowie knife, plucked
the weapon from the scabbard, and, thrusting the captain aside, leaped upon the general with the fury of a madman, hurling him
to the ground and falling headlong upon him
as he lay.   The table was overturned, the
candle extinguished, and they fought blindly
in the darkness. The provost-marshal sprang
to the assistance of his superior officer, and
was himself prostrated upon the struggling
forms.   Curses and inarticulate cries of rage
and pain came from the welter of limbs and
bodies ; the tent came down upon them, and
beneath its hampering and enveloping folds
the struggle went on.   Private Tassman, re-

turning from his errand and dimly conjectur-
ing the situation, threw down his rifle, and,
laying hold of the flouncing canvas at random, vainly tried to drag it off the men under it ; and the sentinel who paced up and
down in front, not daring to leave his beat
though the skies should fall, discharged his
piece.   The report alarmed the camp ; drums
beat the long roll and bugles sounded the as-
sembly, bringing swarms of half-clad men
into the moonlight, dressing as they ran, and
falling into line at the sharp commands of
their officers.   This was well ; being in line
the men were under control ; they stood at
arms while the general's staff and the men
of his escort brought order out of confusion
by lifting off the fallen tent and pulling apart
the breathless and bleeding actors in that
strange contention.

Breathless, indeed, was one : the captain
was dead ; the handle of the bowie knife, protruding from his throat, was pressed back
beneath his chin until the end had caught in
the angle of the jaw, and the hand that delivered the blow had been unable to remove
the weapon.   In the dead man's hand was
his sword, clenched with a grip that defied

the strength of the living. Its blade was streaked with red to the hilt.

Lifted to his feet, the general sank back to the earth with a moan and fainted. Besides his bruises he had two sword-thrusts—one through the thigh, the other through the shoulder.

The spy had suffered the least damage. Apart from a broken right arm, his wounds were such only as might have been incurred in an ordinary combat with nature's weapons. But he was dazed, and seemed hardly to know what had occurred. He shrank away from those attending him, cowered upon the ground, and uttered unintelligible remonstrances. His face, swollen by blows and stained with gouts of blood, nevertheless showed white beneath his dishevelled hair—as white as that of a corpse.

"The man is not insane," said the surgeon in reply to a question; "he is suffering from fright. Who and what is he?"

Private Tassman began to explain. It was the opportunity of his life; he omitted nothing that could in any way accentuate the importance of his own relation to the night's events. When he had finished his story and

was ready to begin it again, nobody gave
him any attention.

The general had now recovered consciousness. He raised himself upon his elbow,
looked about him, and, seeing the spy
crouching by a camp-fire, guarded, said,
simply :

" Take that man to the parade ground and
shoot him."

" The general's mind wanders," said an
officer standing near.

"His mind does *not* wander," the adjutant-
general said. " I have a memorandum from
him about this business ; he had given that
same order to Hasterlick "—with a motion
of the hand toward the dead provost-marshal
—" and, by God ! it shall be executed."

Ten minutes later Sergeant Parker Adderson, of the Federal army, philosopher and
wit, kneeling in the moonlight and begging
incoherently for his life, was shot to death by
twenty men. As the volley rang out upon
the keen air of the winter midnight, General
Clavering, lying white and still in the red
glow of the camp-fire, opened his big blue
eyes, looked pleasantly upon those about
him, and said : " How silent it all is ! "

The surgeon looked at the adjutant-general, gravely and significantly. The patient's eyes slowly closed, and thus he lay for a few moments ; then, his face suffused with a smile of ineffable sweetness, he said, faintly : " I suppose this must be death," and so passed away.

An Affair of Outposts

I

CONCERNING THE WISH TO BE DEAD

TWO men sat in conversation. One was the Governor of the State. The year was 1861 ; the war was on and the Governor already famous for the intelligence and zeal with which he directed all the powers and resources of his State to the service of the Union.

"What! *you?*" the Governor was saying in evident surprise—"you too want a military commission? Really the fifing and drumming must have effected a profound alteration in your convictions. In my character of recruiting sergeant I suppose I ought not to be fastidious, but"— there was a touch of irony in his manner—

"well, have you forgotten that an oath of
allegiance is required?"

"I have altered neither my convictions
nor my sympathies," said the other, tranquilly. "While my sympathies are with
the South, as you do me the honor to recollect, I have never doubted that the North
was in the right. I am a Southerner in fact
and in feeling, but it is my habit in matters
of importance to act as I think, not as I feel."

The Governor was absently tapping his
desk with a pencil; he did not immediately
reply. After a while he said : "I have
heard that there are all kinds of men in the
world, so I suppose there are some like that,
and doubtless you think yourself one. I 've
known you a long time, and—pardon me—
I don't think so."

"Then I am to understand that my application is denied?"

"Unless you can remove my belief that
your Southern sympathies are in some
degree a disqualification, yes. I do not
doubt your good faith, and I know you to
be abundantly fitted by intelligence and
special training for the duties of an officer.
Your convictions, you say, favor the Union

cause, but I prefer a man with his heart in it.   The heart is what men fight with."

"Look here, Governor," said the younger man, with a smile that had more light than warmth :   "I have ' something up my sleeve '—a qualification which I had hoped it would not be necessary to mention.   A great military authority has given a simple recipe for being a good soldier : ' Try always to get yourself killed.'   It is with that purpose that I wish to enter the service. I am not, perhaps, much of a patriot, but I wish to be dead."

The Governor looked at him rather sharply, then a little coldly.   "There are simpler and franker ways," he said.

"In my family, sir," was the reply, "we do not commit suicide—no Armisted has ever done that."

A long silence ensued and neither man looked at the other.   Presently the Governor lifted his eyes from the pencil, which had resumed its tapping, and said :

"Who is she ? "

"My wife."

The Governor tossed the pencil into the desk, rose and walked two or three times across the room. Then he turned to Armisted, who also had risen, looked at him more coldly than before, and said : "But the man—would it not be better that he—could not the country spare him better than it can spare you? Or are the Armisteds opposed to 'the unwritten law'?"

The Armisteds, apparently, could feel an insult : the face of the younger man flushed, then paled, but he subdued himself to the service of his purpose.

"The man's identity is unknown to me," he said, calmly enough.

"Pardon me," said the Governor, with even less of visible contrition than commonly underlies those words. After a moment's reflection he added : "I shall send you to-morrow a captain's commission in the Tenth Infantry, now at Nashville, Tennessee. Good night."

"Good night, sir. I thank you."

Left alone, the Governor remained for a time motionless, leaning against his desk. Presently he shrugged his shoulders as if throwing off a burden. "This is a bad business," he said ; "I don't like it."

Seating himself at a reading-table before

the fire, he took up the book nearest his hand, absently opening it. His eyes fell upon this sentence :

"When God made it necessary for an unfaithful wife to lie about her husband in justification He had the tenderness to endow men with the folly to believe her."

He looked at the title of the book ; it was, *His Excellency the Fool.*

He flung the volume into the fire.

II

HOW TO SAY WHAT IS WORTH HEARING

THE enemy, defeated in two days of battle at Pittsburg Landing, had sullenly retired to Corinth, whence he had come. For manifest incompetence Grant, whose beaten army had been saved from destruction and capture by Buell's soldierly activity and skill, had been relieved of his command, which nevertheless had not been given to Buell, but to Halleck, a man of unproved powers, a theorist, sluggish, irresolute. Foot by foot his troops, always deployed in line of battle to resist the enemy's bickering skirmishes, always entrenching against the columns

that never came, advanced across the thirty
miles of forest and swamp toward an antagonist prepared to vanish at contact, like a
ghost at cock-crow. It was a campaign of
"excursions and alarums," of reconnois-
sances and countermarches, of cross-purposes
and countermanded orders. For weeks the
solemn farce held attention, luring distinguished civilians from fields of political
ambition to see what they safely could of
the horrors of war. Among these was our
friend the Governor. At the headquarters
of the army and in the camps of the troops
from his State he was a familiar figure,
attended by the several members of his
personal staff, showily horsed, faultlessly
betailored, and bravely silk-hatted. Things
of charm they were, rich in suggestions of
peaceful lands beyond a sea of strife. The
bedraggled soldier looked up from his trench
as they passed, leaned upon his spade, and
audibly damned them to signify his sense of
their ornamental irrelevance to the austeri-
ties of his trade.

"I think, Governor," said General Masterson one day, going into informal session
atop of his horse and throwing one leg

across the pommel of his saddle, his favorite
posture—"I think I would not ride any
farther in that direction if I were you.
We 've nothing out there but a line of
skirmishers. That, I presume, is why I
was directed to put these siege guns here :
if the skirmishers are driven in the enemy
will die of dejection at being unable to haul
them away—they 're a trifle heavy."

There is reason to fear that the unstrained
quality of this military humor dropped not
as the gentle rain from heaven upon the
place beneath the civilian's silk hat. Anyhow he abated none of his dignity in recognition.

"I understand," he said, gravely, " that
some of my men are out there—a company
of the Tenth, commanded by Captain Armisted. I should like to meet him if you do
not mind."

"He is worth meeting. But there 's a
bad bit of jungle out there, and I should
advise that you leave your horse and "—
with a look at the Governor's retinue—
"your other impedimenta."

The Governor went forward alone and on
foot. In a half-hour he had pushed through

a tangled undergrowth covering a boggy
soil and entered upon more firm and open
ground. Here he found a half-company of
infantry lounging behind a line of stacked
rifles. The men wore their accoutrements
—their belts, cartridge-boxes, haversacks,
and canteens. Some lying at full length
on the dry leaves were fast asleep : others
in small groups gossiped idly of this and
that ; a few played at cards ; none were far
from the line of stacked arms. To the civilian's eye the scene was one of carelessness,
confusion, indifference ; a soldier would have
observed expectancy and readiness.

At a little distance apart an officer in
fatigue uniform, armed, sat on a fallen tree
noting the approach of the visitor, to whom
a sergeant, rising from one of the groups,
now came forward.

"I wish to see Captain Armisted," said
the Governor.

The sergeant eyed him narrowly, saying
nothing, pointed to the officer, and taking
a rifle from one of the stacks, accompanied
him.

"This man wants to see you, sir," said
the sergeant, saluting. The officer rose.

It would have been a sharp eye that would have recognized him. His hair, which but a few months before had been brown, was streaked with gray. His face, tanned by exposure, was seamed as with age. A long livid scar across the forehead marked the stroke of a sabre; one cheek was drawn and puckered by the work of a bullet. Only a woman of the loyal North would have thought the man handsome.

"Armisted—Captain," said the Governor, extending his hand, "do you not know me?"

"I know you, sir, and I salute you—as the Governor of my State."

Lifting his right hand to the level of his eyes he threw it outward and downward. In the code of military etiquette there is no provision for shaking hands. That of the civilian was withdrawn. If he felt either surprise or chagrin he did not betray it.

"It is the hand that signed your commission," he said.

"And it is the hand—"

The sentence remains unfinished. The sharp report of a rifle came from the front, followed by another and another. A bullet hissed out of the forest and struck a tree near by. The men sprang from the ground, and even before the captain's high, clear voice was done intoning the command "Atten-tion!" had fallen into line in rear of the stacked arms. Again—and now through the din of a crackling fusillade—sounded the strong, deliberate sing-song of authority: "Take . . . arms!" followed by the rattle of unlocking bayonets.

Bullets from the unseen enemy were now flying thick and fast, though mostly well spent and emitting the humming sound which signified interference by twigs and rotation in the plane of flight. Two or three of the men in the line were already struck and down. A few wounded men came limping awkwardly out of the undergrowth from the skirmish line in front ; most of them did not pause, but held their way with white faces and set teeth to the rear.

Suddenly there was a deep, jarring report in front, followed by the startling rush of a shell, which, passing overhead, exploded in the edge of the thicket, setting afire the fallen leaves. Penetrating the din—seeming to float above it, like the melody of a

soaring bird—rang the slow aspirated mono-
tones of the captain's several commands,
without emphasis, without accent, musical
and restful as an even-song under the harvest
moon. Familiar with this tranquillizing
chant in moments of imminent peril, these
raw soldiers of less than a year's training
yielded themselves to the spell, executing its
mandates with the composure and precision
of veterans. Even the distinguished civilian
behind his tree, hesitating between pride
and terror, was accessible to its charm and
contagion. He was conscious of a fortified
resolution, and ran away only when the
skirmishers, under orders to rally on the
reserve, came out of the woods like hunted
hares and formed on the left of the stiff little
line, breathing hard and thankful for the
boon of breath.

III

THE FIGHTING OF ONE WHOSE HEART WAS NOT IN THE QUARREL

Guided in his retreat by that of the
fugitive wounded, the Governor struggled bravely to the rear through the " bad

bit of jungle." He was well winded and a trifle confused. Excepting a single rifle-shot now and again, there was no sound of strife behind him ; the enemy was pulling himself together for a new onset against an antagonist of whose numbers and tactical disposition he was in doubt. The fugitive felt that he would probably be spared to his country, and inly commended the arrangements of Providence to that end, but in leaping a small brook in more open ground one of the arrangements incurred the mischance of a disabling sprain at the ankle. He was unable to continue his flight, for he was too fat to hop, and after several vain attempts causing intolerable pain, seated himself on the earth to nurse his ignoble disability and deprecate the military situation.

A brisk renewal of the firing broke out and stray bullets came flitting and droning by. Then came the crash of two clean, definite volleys, followed by a continuous rattle, through which he heard the yells and cheers of the combatants, punctuated by thunderclaps of cannon. All this told him that Armisted's little command was bitterly beset and fighting at close quarters. The wounded men whom he had distanced began to straggle by on either hand, their numbers visibly augmented by new levies from the line. Singly and by twos and threes, some supporting comrades more desperately hurt than themselves, but all deaf to his own appeals for assistance, they sifted through the underbush and disappeared. The firing was increasingly louder and more distinct, and presently the ailing fugitives were succeeded by men who strode with a firmer tread, occasionally facing about and discharging their pieces, then doggedly resuming their retreat, reloading as they walked. Two or three fell as he looked and lay motionless. One had enough of life left in him to make a pitiful attempt to drag himself to cover. A passing comrade paused beside him long enough to fire, appraised the poor devil's disability with a look, and moved sullenly on, inserting a cartridge in his weapon.

In all this was none of the pomp of war —no hint of glory. Even in his distress and peril the helpless civilian could not forbear to contrast it with the gorgeous parades and reviews held in honor of himself—with the brilliant uniforms, the music, the banners, and the marching. It was an ugly and sickening business : to all that was artistic in his nature revolting, brutal, in bad taste.

"Ugh !" he grunted, shuddering—"this is beastly ! Where is the charm of it all ? Where are the elevated sentiments, the devotion, the heroism, the—"

From a point somewhere near, in the direction of the pursuing enemy, rose the clear, deliberate sing-song of Captain Armisted.

"Stead-y, men—stead-y. Halt ! Commence fir-ing."

The rattle of fewer than a score of rifles could be distinguished through the general uproar, and again that penetrating falsetto :

"Cease fir-ing. In re-treat . . . . maaarch !"

In a few moments this remnant had drifted slowly past the Governor, all to the right of him as they faced in retiring, the men deployed at intervals of a half-dozen paces. At the extreme left and a few yards behind came the captain. The civilian called out his name, but he did not hear. A swarm of

men in gray now broke out of cover in pursuit, making directly for the spot where the
Governor lay—some accident of the ground
had caused them to converge upon that
point : their line had become a crowd. In
a last struggle for life and liberty the Governor attempted to rise, and looking back the
captain saw him. Promptly, but with the
same slow precision as before, he sang his
commands :

" Skirm-ish-ers, halt ! " The men stopped
and according to rule turned to face the
enemy.

" Ral-ly on the right ! "—and they came
in at a run, fixing bayonets and forming
loosely on the man at that end of the line.

" Forward . . to save the Gov-ern-or
of your State . . doub-le quick . . .
maaarch ! "

But one man disobeyed this astonishing
command ! He was dead. With a cheer
they sprang forward over the twenty or
thirty paces between them and their task.
The captain, having a shorter distance to
go, arrived first—simultaneously with the
enemy ! A half-dozen hasty shots were fired
at him, and the foremost man—a fellow

of heroic stature, hatless and bare-breasted
—made a vicious sweep at his head with a
clubbed rifle. The officer parried the blow
at the cost of a broken arm and drove his
sword to the hilt into the giant's breast.
As the body fell the weapon was wrenched
from his hand, and before he could pluck
his revolver from the scabbard at his belt
another man leaped upon him like a tiger,
fastening both hands upon his throat and
bearing him backward upon the prostrate
Governor, still struggling to rise. This
man was promptly spitted upon the bayonet
of a Federal sergeant and his death-gripe
on the captain's throat loosened by a kick
upon each wrist. When the captain had
risen he was at the rear of his men, who had
all passed over and around him and were
thrusting fiercely at their more numerous
but less coherent antagonists. Nearly all
the rifles on both sides were empty and there
was neither time nor opportunity in the crush
to reload. The Confederates were at a dis-
advantage in that most of them lacked bayonets ; they fought by bludgeoning—and a
clubbed rifle is a formidable arm. The
sound of the conflict was a clatter like that

of the interlocking horns of battling bulls—
now and then the pash of a crushed skull,
an oath, or a grunt caused by the impact of
a rifle's muzzle against the abdomen trans-
fixed by its bayonet. Through an opening
made by the fall of one of his men Captain
Armisted sprang, with his dangling left arm,
and in his right hand a full-charged revolver, which he discharged with rapidity
and horrible effect into the thick of the gray
crowd : but across the bodies of the slain
the survivors in the front were pushed forward by their comrades in the rear till
again they breasted the tireless bayonets.
But there were fewer bayonets now to breast
—a beggarly half-dozen, all told. A few
minutes more of this rough work—a little
fighting back to back—and all would be
over.

Suddenly a lively firing was heard on the
right and the left : a fresh line of Federal
skirmishers came forward at a run, driving
before them those parts of the Confederate
line that had been separated by staying the
advance of the centre. And behind these
new and noisy combatants, at a distance
of two or three hundred yards, could be

seen, indistinct among the trees, a line of
battle !

Instinctively before retiring, the crowd in
gray made a tremendous rush upon its hand-
ful of antagonists, overwhelming them by
mere momentum, and, unable to use weapons
in the crush, trampled them, stamped sav-
agely on their limbs, their bodies, their
necks, their faces, then retiring with bloody
feet across its own dead it joined the general
rout and the incident was at an end.

IV

THE GREAT LOVE TO HONOR THE GREAT

THE Governor, who had been unconscious,
opened his eyes and stared about him, slowly
recalling the day's events. A man in the
uniform of a major was kneeling beside him;
he was a surgeon. Grouped about were the
civilian members of the gubernatorial staff,
their faces expressing a natural solicitude
regarding their offices. A little apart stood
General Masterson chatting with another
officer and gesticulating with a cigar. He
was saying : "It was the beautifulest fight
ever made—by God, sir, it was great ! "

The beauty and greatness were attested by a row of dead, trimly disposed, and another of wounded, less formally placed, restless, half naked, but bravely bebandaged.

"How do you feel, sir?" said the surgeon. "I find no wound."

. "I think I am all right," the patient replied, sitting up. "It is that ankle."

The surgeon transferred his attention to the ankle, cutting away the boot. All eyes followed the knife.

In moving the leg a folded paper was uncovered. The patient picked it up and carelessly opened it. It was a letter three months old, signed "Julia." Catching sight of his name in it he read it. It was nothing very remarkable—merely a weak wife's confession of unprofitable sin—the penitence of a deserted mistress. The letter had fallen from the pocket of Captain Armisted ; the reader quietly transferred it to his own.

An aide-de-camp rode up and dismounted. Advancing to the Governor he saluted.

"Sir," he said, "I am sorry to find you wounded—the Commanding General has not been informed. He presents his compliments, and I am directed to say that he has

ordered for to-morrow a grand review of the
reserve corps in your honor. I venture to
add that the General's carriage is at your
service if you are able to attend."

" Be pleased to say to the Commanding
General that I am deeply touched by his
kindness. If you have the patience to wait
a few moments you shall convey a more definite reply."

He smiled brightly and glancing at the
surgeon and his assistants added : " At present—if you will permit an allusion to the
horrors of peace—I am ' in the hands of my
friends.' "

The humor of the great is infectious ; all
laughed who heard.

" Where is Captain Armisted ? " the Governor asked, not altogether carelessly.

The surgeon looked up from his work,
pointing silently to the nearest body in the
row of dead, the features discreetly covered
with a handkerchief. It lay so near that
the great man could have laid his hand upon
it, but he did not. He may have feared that
it would bleed.

Civilians

A Watcher by the Dead

I

IN an upper room of an unoccupied dwelling in that part of San Francisco known as North Beach lay the body of a man, under a sheet. The hour was near nine in the evening ; the room was dimly lighted by a single candle. . Although the weather was warm, the two windows, contrary to the custom which gives the dead plenty of air, were closed and the blinds drawn down. The furniture of the room consisted of but three pieces,—an arm-chair, a small reading-stand supporting the candle, and a long kitchen table, supporting the body of the man. All these, as also the corpse, would seem to have been recently brought in, for an observer, had there been one, would have seen that all were free from dust, whereas everything else in the room was pretty thickly coated with it, and there were cobwebs in the angles of the walls.

Under the sheet the outlines of the body could be traced, even the features, these having that unnaturally sharp definition which seems to belong to faces of the dead, but is really characteristic of those only that have been wasted by disease. From the silence of the room one would rightly have inferred that it was not in the front of the house, facing a street. It really faced nothing but a high breast of rock, the rear of the building being set into a hill.

As a neighboring church clock was striking nine with an indolence which seemed to imply such an indifference to the flight of time that one could hardly help wondering why it took the trouble to strike at all, the single door of the room was opened and a man entered, advancing toward the body. As he did so the door closed, apparently of its own volition ; there was a grating, as of a key turned with difficulty, and the snap of the lock bolt as it shot into its socket. A sound of retiring footsteps in the passage outside ensued, and the man was, to all ap-

pearance, a prisoner. Advancing to the
table, he stood a moment looking down at
the body ; then, with a slight shrug of the
shoulders, walked over to one of the windows and hoisted the blind. The darkness
outside was absolute, the panes were covered with dust, but, by wiping this away,
he could see that the window was fortified
with strong iron bars crossing it within a
few inches of the glass, and imbedded in
the masonry on each side. He examined
the other window. It was the same. He
manifested no great curiosity in the matter,
did not even so much as raise the sash. If
he was a prisoner he was apparently a trac-
table one. Having completed his examination of the room, he seated himself in the
arm-chair, took a book from his pocket,
drew the stand with its candle alongside,
and began to read.

The man was young — not more than
thirty—dark in complexion, smooth-shaven,
with brown hair. His face was thin and
high-nosed, with a broad forehead and a
" firmness " of the chin and jaw which is said
by those having it to denote resolution.
The eyes were gray and steadfast, not mov-

ing except with definitive purpose. They were now for the greater part of the time fixed upon his book, but he occasionally withdrew them and turned them to the body on the table, not, apparently, from any dismal fascination which, under such circumstances, it might be supposed to exercise upon even a courageous person, nor with a conscious rebellion against the opposite influence which might dominate a timid one. He looked at it as if in his reading he had come upon something recalling him to a sense of his surroundings. Clearly this watcher by the dead was discharging his trust with intelligence and composure, as became him.

After reading for perhaps a half-hour he seemed to come to the end of a chapter and quietly laid away the book. He then rose, and, taking the reading-stand from the floor, carried it into a corner of the room near one of the windows, lifted the candle from it, and returned to the empty fireplace before which he had been sitting.

A moment later he walked over to the body on the table, lifted the sheet, and turned it back from the head, exposing a mass of dark hair and a thin face-cloth, beneath which the features showed with even sharper definition than before. Shading his eyes by interposing his free hand between them and the candle, he stood looking at his motionless companion with a serious and tranquil regard. Satisfied with his inspection, he pulled the sheet over the face again, and, returning to his chair, took some matches off the candlestick, put them in the side pocket of his sack-coat, and sat down. He then lifted the candle from its socket and looked at it critically, as if calculating how long it would last. It was barely two inches long ; in another hour he would be in darkness. He replaced it in the candlestick and blew it out.

II

In a physician's office in Kearny Street three men sat about a table, drinking punch and smoking. It was late in the evening, almost midnight, indeed, and there had been no lack of punch. The eldest of the three, Dr. Helberson, was the host—it was in his rooms they sat. He was about thirty

years of age ; the others were even younger ;
all were physicians.

"The superstitious awe with which the
living regard the dead," said Dr. Helberson, "is hereditary and incurable. One
needs no more be ashamed of it than of the
fact that he inherits, for example, an inca-
pacity for mathematics, or a tendency to lie."

The others laughed. "Ought n't a man
to be ashamed to lie ? " asked the youngest
of the three, who was, in fact, a medical
student not yet graduated.

"My dear Harper, I said nothing about
that. The tendency to lie is one thing ;
lying is another."

"But do you think," said the third man,
"that this superstitious feeling, this fear of
the dead, reasonless as we know it to be, is
universal? I am myself not conscious of it."

"Oh, but it is 'in your system' for all
that," replied Helberson ; "it needs only
the right conditions — what Shakespeare
calls the ' confederate season '—to manifest
itself in some very disagreeable way that
will open your eyes. Physicians and soldiers are, of course, more nearly free from it
than others."

"Physicians and soldiers!—why don't you add hangmen and headsmen? Let us have in all the assassin classes."

"No, my dear Mancher; the juries will not let the public executioners acquire sufficient familiarity with death to be altogether unmoved by it."

Young Harper, who had been helping himself to a fresh cigar at the sideboard, resumed his seat. "What would you consider conditions under which any man of woman born would become insupportably conscious of his share of our common weakness in this regard?" he asked, rather verbosely.

"Well, I should say that if a man were locked up all night with a corpse—alone—in a dark room—of a vacant house—with no bed covers to pull over his head—and lived through it without going altogether mad—he might justly boast himself not of woman born, nor yet, like Macduff, a product of Cæsarean section."

"I thought you never would finish piling up conditions," said Harper, "but I know a man who is neither a physician nor a soldier who will accept them all, for any stake you like to name."

"Who is he?"

"His name is Jarette—a stranger in California; comes from my town in New York. I have no money to back him, but he will back himself with dead loads of it."

"How do you know that?"

"He would rather bet than eat. As for fear—I dare say he thinks it some cutaneous disorder, or, possibly, a particular kind of religious heresy."

"What does he look like?" Helberson was evidently becoming interested.

"Like Mancher, here—might be his twin brother."

"I accept the challenge," said Helberson, promptly.

"Awfully obliged to you for the compliment, I'm sure," drawled Mancher, who was growing sleepy. "Can't I get into this?"

"Not against me," Helberson said. "I don't want *your* money."

"All right," said Mancher; "I'll be the corpse."

The others laughed.

The outcome of this crazy conversation we have seen.

III

In extinguishing his meagre allowance of
candle Mr. Jarette's object was to preserve
it against some unforeseen need. He may
have thought, too, or half thought, that the
darkness would be no worse at one time than
another, and if the situation became insupportable, it would be better to have a means
of relief, or even release. At any rate, it
was wise to have a little reserve of light, even
if only to enable him to look at his watch.

No sooner had he blown out the candle
and set it on the floor at his side than he settled himself comfortably in the arm-chair,
leaned back and closed his eyes, hoping and
expecting to sleep. In this he was disap-
pointed; he had never in his life felt less
sleepy, and in a few minutes he gave up the
attempt. But what could he do? He could
not go groping about in the absolute darkness at the risk of bruising himself—at the
risk, too, of blundering against the table and
rudely disturbing the dead. We all recognize their right to lie at rest, with immunity
from all that is harsh and violent. Jarette
almost succeeded in making himself believe

that considerations of that kind restrained
him from risking the collision and fixed him
to the chair.

While thinking of this matter he fancied
that he heard a faint sound in the direction
of the table—what kind of sound he could
hardly have explained.   He did not turn his
head.   Why should he—in the darkness?
But he listened—why should he not?   And
listening he grew giddy and grasped the
arms of the chair for support.   There was a
strange ringing in his ears ; his head seemed
bursting ; his chest was oppressed by the
constriction of his clothing.   He wondered
why it was so, and whether these were
symptoms of fear.   Suddenly, with a long
and strong expiration, his chest appeared to
collapse, and with the great gasp with which
he refilled his exhausted lungs the vertigo
left him, and he knew that so intently had
he listened that he had held his breath almost to suffocation.   The revelation was
vexatious ; he arose, pushed away the chair
with his foot, and strode to the centre of the
room.   But one does not stride far in darkness ; he began to grope, and, finding the
wall, followed it to an angle, turned, fol-

lowed it past the two windows, and there in another corner came into violent contact with the reading-stand, overturning it. It made a clatter that startled him. He was annoyed. " How the devil could I have forgotten where it was ! " he muttered, and groped his way along the third wall to the fireplace. " I must put things to rights," said Mr. Jarette, feeling the floor for the candle.

Having recovered that, he lighted it and instantly turned his eyes to the table, where, naturally, nothing had undergone any change. The reading-stand lay unobserved upon the floor : he had forgotten to " put it to rights." He looked all about the room, dispersing the deeper shadows by movements of the candle in his hand, and, crossing over to the door, tested it by turning and pulling the knob with all his strength. It did not yield and this seemed to afford him a certain satisfaction ; indeed, he secured it more firmly by a bolt which he had not before observed. Returning to his chair, he looked at his watch ; it was half-past nine. With a start of surprise he held the watch at his ear. It had not stopped.

The candle was now visibly shorter. He again extinguished it, placing it on the floor at his side as before.

Mr. Jarette was not at his ease ; he was distinctly dissatisfied with his surroundings, and with himself for being so. "What have I to fear?" he thought. "This is ridiculous and disgraceful; I will not be so great a fool." But courage does not come of saying, "I will be courageous," nor of recognizing its appropriateness to the occasion. The more Jarette condemned himself, the more reason he gave himself for condemnation ; the greater the number of variations which he played upon the simple theme of the harmlessness of the dead, the more insupportable grew the discord of his emotions. "What!" he cried aloud in the anguish of his spirit, "what ! shall I, who have not a shade of superstition in my nature—I, who have no belief in immortality —I, who know (and never more clearly than now) that the after-life is the dream of a desire—shall I lose at once my bet, my honor, and my self-respect, perhaps my reason, because certain savage ancestors, dwelling in caves and burrows, conceived the monstrous

notion that the dead walk by night ; that—"
Distinctly, unmistakably, Mr. Jarette heard
behind him a light, soft sound of footfalls,
deliberate, regular, and successively nearer !

IV

Just before daybreak the next morning
Dr. Helberson and his young friend Harper
were driving slowly through the streets of
North Beach in the doctor's coupé.

" Have you still the confidence of youth in
the courage or stolidity of your friend ? "
said the elder man. " Do you believe that
I have lost this wager ? "

" I *know* you have," replied the other,
with enfeebling emphasis.

" Well, upon my soul, I hope so."

It was spoken earnestly, almost solemnly.
There was a silence for a few moments.

" Harper," the doctor resumed, looking
very serious in the shifting half-lights that
entered the carriage as they passed the street
lamps, " I don't feel altogether comfortable
about this business. If your friend had not
irritated me by the contemptuous manner in
which he treated my doubt of his endurance
—a purely physical quality—and by the cool

incivility of his suggestion that the corpse be that of a physician, I should not have gone on with it. If anything should happen, we are ruined, as I fear we deserve to be."

"What can happen? Even if the matter should be taking a serious turn, of which I am not at all afraid, Mancher has only to 'resurrect' himself and explain matters. With a genuine 'subject' from the dissecting-room, or one of your late patients, it might be different."

Dr. Mancher, then, had been as good as his promise ; he was the "corpse."

Dr. Helberson was silent for a long time, as the carriage, at a snail's pace, crept along the same street it had travelled two or three times already. Presently he spoke : "Well, let us hope that Mancher, if he has had to rise from the dead, has been discreet about it. A mistake in that might make matters worse instead of better."

"Yes," said Harper, "Jarette would kill him. But, Doctor "—looking at his watch as the carriage passed a gas lamp—" it is nearly four o'clock at last."

A moment later the two had quitted the vehicle, and were walking briskly toward the

long-unoccupied house belonging to the doctor in which they had immured Mr. Jarette,
in accordance with the terms of the mad
wager. As they neared it, they met a man
running. "Can you tell me," he cried, suddenly checking his speed, " where I can find
a physician ? "

" What 's the matter ? " Helberson asked,
non-committal.

" Go and see for yourself," said the man,
resuming his running.

They hastened on. Arrived at the house,
they saw several persons entering in haste
and excitement. In some of the dwellings
near by and across the way, the chamber
windows were thrown up, showing a protru-
sion of heads. All heads were asking questions, none heeding the questions of the
others. A few of the windows with closed
blinds were illuminated ; the inmates of those
rooms were dressing to come down. Exactly opposite the door of the house which
they sought, a street lamp threw a yellow,
insufficient light upon the scene, seeming to
say that it could disclose a good deal more
if it wished. Harper, who was now deathly
pale, paused at the door and laid a hand

upon his companion's arm. " It is all up
with us, Doctor," he said in extreme agita-
tion, which contrasted strangely with his
free-and-easy words ; " the game has gone
against us all. Let 's not go in there ; I 'm
for lying low."

" I 'm a physician," said Dr. Helberson,
calmly ; " there may be need of one."

They mounted the doorsteps and were
about to enter. The door was open ; the
street lamp opposite lighted the passage into which it opened. It was full of people.
Some had ascended the stairs at the farther
end, and, denied admittance above, waited
for better fortune. All were talking, none
listening. Suddenly, on the upper landing
there was a great commotion ; a man had
sprung out of a door and was breaking away
from those endeavoring to detain him. Down
through the mass of affrighted idlers he
came, pushing them aside, flattening them
against the wall on one side, or compelling
them to cling to the rail on the other, clutching them by the throat, striking them sav-
agely, thrusting them back down the stairs,
and walking over the fallen. His clothing
was in disorder, he was without a hat. His

eyes, wild and restless, had in them something more terrifying than his apparently superhuman strength. His face, smooth-shaven, was bloodless, his hair snow-white.

As the crowd at the foot of the stairs, having more freedom, fell away to let him pass, Harper sprang forward. "Jarette! Jarette!" he cried.

Dr. Helberson seized Harper by the collar and dragged him back. The man looked into their faces without seeming to see them, and sprang through the door, down the steps, into the street, and away. A stout policeman, who had had inferior success in conquering his way down the stairway, followed a moment later and started in pursuit, all the heads in the windows—those of women and children now—screaming in guidance.

The stairway being now partly cleared, most of the crowd having rushed down to the street to observe the flight and pursuit, Dr. Helberson mounted to the landing, followed by Harper. At a door in the upper passage an officer denied them admittance. "We are physicians," said the doctor, and they passed in. The room was full of men, dimly seen, crowded about a table. The newcomers edged their way forward, and looked over the shoulders of those in the front rank. Upon the table, the lower limbs covered with a sheet, lay the body of a man, brilliantly illuminated by the beam of a bull's-eye lantern held by a policeman standing at the feet. The others, excepting those near the head—the officer himself—all were in darkness. The face of the body showed yellow, repulsive, horrible ! The eyes were partly open and upturned, and the jaw fallen; traces of froth defiled the lips, the chin, the cheeks. A tall man, evidently a physician, bent over the body with his hand thrust under the shirt front. He withdrew it and placed two fingers in the open mouth. " This man has been about two hours dead," said he. " It is a case for the coroner."

He drew a card from his pocket, handed it to the officer, and made his way toward the door.

" Clear the room—out, all !" said the officer, sharply, and the body disappeared as if it had been snatched away, as shifting the lantern he flashed its beam of light here and there against the faces of the crowd. The effect was amazing ! The men, blinded, confused, almost terrified, made a tumultuous rush for the door, pushing, crowding, and tumbling over one another as they fled, like the hosts of Night before the shafts of Apollo. Upon the struggling, trampling mass the officer poured his light without pity and without cessation. Caught in the current, Helberson and Harper were swept out of the room and cascaded down the stairs into the street.

"Good God, Doctor ! did I not tell you that Jarette would kill him ? " said Harper, as soon as they were clear of the crowd.

"I believe you did," replied the other, without apparent emotion.

They walked on in silence, block after block. Against the graying east the dwellings of our hill tribes showed in silhouette. The familiar milk wagon was already astir in the streets ; the baker's man would soon come upon the scene ; the newspaper carrier was abroad in the land.

"It strikes me, youngster," said Helberson, " that you and I have been having too much of the morning air lately. It is unwholesome ; we need a change. What do you say to a tour in Europe ? "

" When ? "

" I 'm not particular. I should suppose that four o'clock this afternoon would be early enough."

" I 'll meet you at the boat," said Harper.

V

Seven years afterward these two men sat upon a bench in Madison Square, New York, in familiar conversation. Another man, who had been observing them for some time, himself unobserved, approached and, courteously lifting his hat from locks as white as snow, said : " I beg your pardon, gentlemen, but when you have killed a man by coming to life, it is best to change clothes with him, and at the first opportunity make a break for liberty."

Helberson and Harper exchanged significant glances. They were apparently amused. The former then looked the stranger kindly in the eye, and replied :

" That has always been my plan. I entirely agree with you as to its advant—"

He stopped suddenly and grew deathly pale. He stared at the man, open-mouthed; he trembled visibly.

"Ah!" said the stranger, "I see that you are indisposed, Doctor. If you cannot treat yourself, Dr. Harper can do something for you, I am sure."

"Who the devil are you?" said Harper, bluntly.

The stranger came nearer, and, bending toward them, said in a whisper: "I call myself Jarette sometimes, but I don't mind telling you, for old friendship, that I am Dr. William Mancher."

The revelation brought both men to their feet. "Mancher!" they cried in a breath; and Helberson added: "It is true, by God!"

"Yes," said the stranger, smiling vaguely, "it is true enough, no doubt."

He hesitated, and seemed to be trying to recall something, then began humming a popular air. He had apparently forgotten their presence.

"Look here, Mancher," said the elder of the two, "tell us just what occurred that night—to Jarette, you know."

"Oh, yes, about Jarette," said the other. "It's odd I should have neglected to tell you—I tell it so often. You see I knew, by overhearing him talking to himself, that he was pretty badly frightened. So I could n't resist the temptation to come to life and have a bit of fun out of him—I could n't, really. That was all right, though certainly I did not think he would take it so seriously ; I did not, truly. And afterward—well, it was a tough job changing places with him, and then—damn you ! you did n't let me out !"

Nothing could exceed the ferocity with which these last words were delivered. Both men stepped back in alarm.

"We ?—why—why," Helberson stammered, losing his self-possession utterly, "we had nothing to do with it."

"Did n't I say you were Drs. Hellborn and Sharper ?" inquired the lunatic, laughing.

"My name is Helberson, yes ; and this gentleman is Mr. Harper," replied the former, reassured. "But we are not physicians now ; we are—well, hang it, old man, we are gamblers."

And that was the truth.

"A very good profession — very good, indeed ; and, by the way, I hope Sharper here paid over Jarette's money like an honest stakeholder. A very good and honorable profession," he repeated, thoughtfully, moving carelessly away ; "but I stick to the old one. I am High Supreme Medical Officer of the Bloomingdale Asylum ; it is my duty to cure the superintendent."

The Man and the Snake

It is of veritabyll report, and attested of so many that there be nowe of wyse and learned none to gaynsaye it, that y^e serpente hys eye hath a magnetick propertie that whosoe falleth into its svasion is drawn forwards in despyte of his wille, and perisheth miserabyll by ye creature hys byte.

STRETCHED at ease upon a sofa, in gown and slippers, Harker Brayton smiled as he read the foregoing sentence in old Morryster's *Marvells of Science.* "The only marvel in the matter," he said to himself, "is that the wise and learned in Morryster's day should have believed such nonsense as is rejected by most of even the ignorant in ours."

A train of reflection followed—for Brayton was a man of thought—and he unconsciously lowered his book without altering the direction of his eyes. As soon as the

volume had gone below the line of sight,
something in an obscure corner of the room
recalled his attention to his surroundings.
What he saw, in the shadow under his bed,
were two small points of light, apparently
about an inch apart. They might have been
reflections of the gas jet above him, in mental
nail heads ; he gave them but little thought
and resumed his reading. A moment later
something—some impulse which it did not
occur to him to analyze—impelled him to
lower the book again and seek for what he
saw before. The points of light were still
there. They seemed to have become brighter
than before, shining with a greenish lustre
which he had not at first observed. He
thought, too, that they might have moved a
trifle—were somewhat nearer. They were
still too much in shadow, however, to reveal
their nature and origin to an indolent attention, and he resumed his reading. Suddenly
something in the text suggested a thought
which made him start and drop the book for
the third time to the side of the sofa, whence,
escaping from his hand, it fell sprawling to
the floor, back upward. Brayton, half-risen,
was staring intently into the obscurity

beneath the bed, where the points of light
shone with, it seemed to him, an added fire.
His attention was now fully aroused, his gaze
eager and imperative. It disclosed, almost
directly beneath the foot-rail of the bed, the
coils of a large serpent—the points of light
were its eyes ! Its horrible head, thrust flatly
forth from the innermost coil and resting
upon the outermost, was directed straight
toward him, the definition of the wide,
brutal jaw and the idiot-like forehead serving to show the direction of its malevolent
gaze. The eyes were no longer merely
luminous points ; they looked into his own
with a meaning, a malign significance.

II

A snake in a bedroom of a modern city
dwelling of the better sort is, happily, not
so common a phenomenon as to make explanation altogether needless. Harker Brayton, a bachelor of thirty-five, a scholar, idler,
and something of an athlete, rich, popular,
and of sound health, had returned to San
Francisco from all manner of remote and
unfamiliar countries. His tastes, always a

trifle luxurious, had taken on an added
exuberance from long privation ; and the
resources of even the Castle Hotel being
inadequate to their perfect gratification, he
had gladly accepted the hospitality of his
friend, Dr. Druring, the distinguished scientist. Dr. Druring's house, a large, old-
fashioned one in what was now an obscure
quarter of the city, had an outer and visible
aspect of proud reserve. It plainly would
not associate with the contiguous elements
of its altered environment, and appeared to
have developed some of the eccentricities
which come of isolation. One of these was
a " wing," conspicuously irrelevant in point
of architecture, and no less rebellious in the
matter of purpose ; for it was a combination
of laboratory, menagerie, and museum. It
was here that the doctor indulged the scientific side of his nature in the study of such
forms of animal life as engaged his interest
and comforted his taste—which, it must be
confessed, ran rather to the lower types.
For one of the higher nimbly and sweetly
to recommend itself unto his gentle senses,
it had at least to retain certain rudimentary
characteristics allying it to such " dragons

of the prime" as toads and snakes. His scientific sympathies were distinctly reptilian; he loved nature's vulgarians and described himself as the Zola of zoölogy. His wife and daughters not having the advantage to share his enlightened curiosity regarding the works and ways of our ill-starred fellow-creatures, were, with needless austerity, excluded from what he called the Snakery and doomed to companionship with their own kind, though, to soften the rigors of their lot, he had permitted them, out of his great wealth, to outdo the reptiles in the gorgeousness of their surroundings and to shine with a superior splendor.

Architecturally, and in point of "furnishing," the Snakery had a severe simplicity befitting the humble circumstances of its occupants, many of whom, indeed, could not safely have been intrusted with the liberty which is necessary to the full enjoyment of luxury, for they had the troublesome peculiarity of being alive. In their own apartments, however, they were under as little personal restraint as was compatible with their protection from the baneful habit of swallowing one another; and, as Brayton

had thoughtfully been apprised, it was more
than a tradition that some of them had at
divers times been found in parts of the premises where it would have embarrassed them
to explain their presence. Despite the Snakery and its uncanny associations—to which,
indeed, he gave little attention—Brayton
found life at the Druring mansion very much
to his mind.

III

Beyond a smart shock of surprise and a
shudder of mere loathing, Mr. Brayton was
not greatly affected. His first thought was
to ring the call bell and bring a servant;
but, although the bell cord dangled within
easy reach, he made no movement toward
it; it had occurred to his mind that the act
might subject him to the suspicion of fear,
which he certainly did not feel. He was
more keenly conscious of the incongruous
nature of the situation than affected by its
perils; it was revolting, but absurd.

The reptile was of a species with which
Brayton was unfamiliar. Its length he
could only conjecture; the body at the
largest visible part seemed about as thick as

his forearm. In what way was it dangerous,
if in any way? Was it venomous? Was it a
constrictor?   His knowledge of nature's
danger signals did not enable him to say;
he had never deciphered the code.   .

If not dangerous, the creature was at least
offensive. It was *de trop*—" matter out of
place " —an impertinence. The gem was
unworthy of the setting. Even the barbarous taste of our time and country, which
had loaded the walls of the room with pictures, the floor with furniture and the furniture with bric-a-brac, had not quite fitted
the place for this bit of the savage life of
the jungle. Besides—insupportablethought!
—the exhalations of its breath mingled
with the atmosphere which he himself was
breathing.

These thoughts shaped themselves with
greater or less definition in Brayton's mind,
and begot action. The process is what we
call consideration and decision. It is thus
that we are wise and unwise. It is thus that
the withered leaf in an autumn breeze shows
greater or less intelligence than its fellows,
falling upon the land or upon the lake.
The secret of human action is an open one :

something contracts our muscles. Does it
matter if we give to the preparatory molecu-
lar changes the name of will?

Brayton rose to his feet and prepared to
back softly away from the snake, without
disturbing it, if possible, and through the
door. People retire so from the presence of
the great, for greatness is power, and power
is a menace. He knew that he could walk
backward without error. Should the mon-
ster follow, the taste which had plastered
the walls with paintings had consistently
supplied a rack of murderous Oriental weapons from which he could snatch one to
suit the occasion. In the meantime the
snake's eyes burned with a more pitiless
malevolence than ever.

Brayton lifted his right foot free of the
floor to step backward. That moment he
felt a strong aversion to doing so.

" I am accounted brave," he murmured ;
" is bravery, then, no more than pride ? Because there are none to witness the shame
shall I retreat ?"

He was steadying himself with his right
hand upon the back of a chair, his foot suspended.

"Nonsense!" he said aloud; "I am not so great a coward as to fear to seem to myself afraid."

He lifted the foot a little higher by slightly bending the knee, and thrust it sharply to the floor—an inch in front of the other! He could not think how that occurred. A trial with the left foot had the same result; it was again in advance of the right. The hand upon the chair back was grasping it; the arm was straight, reaching somewhat backward. One might have said that he was reluctant to lose his hold. The snake's malignant head was still thrust forth from the inner coil as before, the neck level. It had not moved, but its eyes were now electric sparks, radiating an infinity of luminous needles.

The man had an ashy pallor. Again he took a step forward, and another, partly dragging the chair, which when finally released, fell upon the floor with a crash. The man groaned; the snake made neither sound nor motion, but its eyes were two dazzling suns. The reptile itself was wholly concealed by them. They gave off enlarging rings of rich and vivid colors, which at their greatest expansion successively vanished like soap bubbles ; they seemed to approach his very face, and anon were an immeasurable distance away. He heard, somewhere, the continuous throbbing of a great drum, with desultory bursts of far music, inconceivably sweet, like the tones of an æolian harp. He knew it for the sunrise melody of Memnon's statue, and thought he stood in the Nileside reeds hearing, with exalted sense, that immortal anthem through the silence of the centuries.

The music ceased ; rather, it became by insensible degrees the distant roll of a retreating thunder-storm. A landscape, glittering with sun and rain, stretched before him, arched with a vivid rainbow, framing in its giant curve a hundred visible cities. In the middle distance a vast serpent, wearing a crown, reared its head out of its voluminous convolutions and looked at him with his dead mother's eyes. Suddenly this enchanting landscape seemed to rise swiftly upward, like the drop scene at a theatre, and vanished in a blank. Something struck him a hard blow upon the face and breast. He had fallen to the floor ;

the blood ran from his broken nose and his
bruised lips. For a time he was dazed and
stunned, and lay with closed eyes, his face
against the floor. In a few moments he had
recovered, and then knew that his fall, by
withdrawing his eyes, had broken the spell
which held him. He felt that now, by keeping his gaze averted, he would be able to
retreat. But the thought of the serpent
within a few feet of his head, yet unseen—
perhaps in the very act of springing upon
him and throwing its coils about his throat
—was too horrible! He lifted his head,
stared again into those baleful eyes, and
was again in bondage.

The snake had not moved, and appeared
somewhat to have lost its power upon the
imagination; the gorgeous illusions of a
few moments before were not repeated.
Beneath that flat and brainless brow its
black, beady eyes simply glittered, as at first,
with an expression unspeakably malignant.
It was as if the creature, assured of its
triumph, had determined to practice no more
alluring wiles.

Now ensued a fearful scene. The man,
prone upon the floor, within a yard of his

enemy, raised the upper part of his body
upon his elbows, his head thrown back, his
legs extended to their full length.   His face
was white between its stains of blood ; his
eyes were strained open to their uttermost
expansion.   There was froth upon his lips ;
it dropped off in flakes.   Strong convulsions
ran through his body, making almost serpen-
tine undulations.   He bent himself at the
waist, shifting his legs from side to side.
And every movement left him a little nearer
to the snake.   He thrust his hands forward
to brace himself back, yet constantly advanced upon his elbows.

IV

Dr. Druring and his wife sat in the library.
The scientist was in rare good humor.

"I have just obtained, by exchange with
another collector," he said, "a splendid
specimen of the *ophiophagus*."

"And what may that be ?" the lady inquired with a somewhat languid enterest.

"Why, bless my soul. what profound ignorance !   My dear, a man who ascertains
after marriage that his wife does not know

Greek, is entitled to a divorce. The *ophiophagus* is a snake which eats other snakes."

" I hope it will eat all yours," she said,
absently shifting the lamp.   " But how does
it get the other snakes ? By charming them,
I suppose."

" That is just like you, dear," said the
doctor, with an affectation of petulance.
" You know how irritating to me is any
allusion to that vulgar superstition about
the snake's power of fascination."

The conversation was interrupted by a
mighty cry, which rang through the silent
house like the voice of a demon shouting in
a tomb ! Again and yet again it sounded,
with terrible distinctness. They sprang to
their feet, the man confused, the lady pale
and speechless with fright. Almost before
the echoes of the last cry had died away,
the doctor was out of the room, springing up
the stairs two steps at a time. In the corri-
dor, in front of Brayton's chamber, he met
some servants who had come from the upper
floor. Together they rushed at the door
without knocking. It was unfastened and
gave way. Brayton lay upon his stomach
on the floor, dead. His head and arms were

partly concealed under the foot rail of the bed. They pulled the body away, turning it upon the back. The face was daubed with blood and froth, the eyes were wide open, staring—a dreadful sight !

"Died in a fit," said the scientist, bending his knee and placing his hand upon the heart. While in that position, he happened to glance under the bed. "Good God !" he added, "how did this thing get in here ?"

He reached under the bed, pulled out the snake, and flung it, still coiled, to the center of the room, whence, with a harsh, shuffling sound, it slid across the polished floor till stopped by the wall, where it lay without motion. It was a stuffed snake ; its eyes were two shoe buttons.

A Holy Terror

I

THERE was an entire lack of interest in the latest arrival at Hurdy-Gurdy. He was not even christened with the picturesquely descriptive nickname which is so frequently a mining camp's word of welcome to the newcomer. In almost any other camp thereabout this circumstance would of itself have secured him some such appellation as " The White-headed Conundrum," or " No Sarvey "—an expression naively supposed to suggest to quick intelligences the Spanish *quien sabe*. He came without provoking a ripple of concern upon the social surface of Hurdy-Gurdy—a place which, to the general Californian contempt of men's personal antecedents superadded a local indifference of its own. The time was long past when it was of any importance who came there, or if anybody came. No one was living at Hurdy-Gurdy.

Two years before, the camp had boasted a stirring population of two or three thousand males, and not fewer than a dozen females. A majority of the former had done a few weeks' earnest work in demonstrating, to the disgust of the latter, the singularly mendacious character of the person whose ingenious tales of rich gold deposits had lured them thither—work, by the way, in which there was as little mental satisfaction as pecuniary profit ; for a bullet from the pistol of a public-spirited citizen had put that imaginative gentleman beyond the reach of aspersion on the third day of the camp's existence. Still, his fiction had a certain foundation in fact, and many had lingered a considerable time in and about Hurdy-Gurdy, though now all had been long gone.

But they had left ample evidence of their sojourn. From the point where Injun Creek falls into the Rio San Juan Smith, up along both banks of the former into the cañon whence it emerges, extended a double row of forlorn shanties that seemed about to fall upon one another's neck to bewail their desolation ; while about an equal number appeared to have straggled up the slope on either hand, and perched themselves upon commanding eminences, whence they craned forward to get a good view of the affecting scene. Most of these habitations were emaciated, as by famine, to the condition of mere skeletons, about which clung unlovely tatters of what might have been skin, but was really canvas. The little valley itself, torn and gashed by pick and shovel, was unhandsome with long, bending lines of decaying flume resting here and there upon the summits of sharp ridges, and stilting awkwardly across the intervals upon unhewn poles. The whole place presented that raw and forbidding aspect of arrested development which is a new country's substitute for the solemn grace of ruin wrought by time. Wherever there remained a patch of the original soil, a rank overgrowth of weeds and brambles had spread upon the scene, and from its dank, unwholesome shades the visitor curious in such matters might have obtained numberless souvenirs of the camp's former glory—fellowless boots mantled with green mould and plethoric of rotting leaves ; an occasional old felt hat ; desultory remnants of a flannel shirt ; sardine boxes inhumanly mutilated, and a surprising profusion of black bottles, distributed with a truly catholic impartiality, everywhere.

II

The man who had now rediscovered Hurdy-Gurdy was evidently not curious as to its archæology. Nor, as he looked about him upon the dismal evidences of wasted work and broken hopes, their dispiriting significance accentuated by the ironical pomp of a cheap gilding by the rising sun, did he supplement his sigh of weariness by one of sensibility. He simply removed from the back of his tired burro a miner's outfit a trifle larger than the animal itself, picketed that creature, and, selecting a hatchet from his kit, moved off at once across the dry bed of Injun Creek to the top of a low, gravelly hill beyond.

Stepping across a prostrate fence of brush and boards, he picked up one of the latter split it into five parts, and sharpened them at one end. He then began a kind of search, occasionally stooping to examine something with close attention. At last his patient scrutiny appeared to be rewarded with success, for he suddenly erected his figure to its full height, made a gesture of satisfaction, pronounced the word "Scarry," and at once strode away, with long, equal steps, which he counted, then stopped and drove one of his stakes into the earth. He then looked carefully about him, measured off a number of paces over a singularly uneven ground, and hammered in another. Pacing off twice the distance at a right angle to his former course, he drove down a third, and repeating the process, sank home the fourth, and then a fifth. This he split at the top, and in the cleft inserted an old letter envelope, covered with an intricate system of pencil tracks. In short, he staked off a hill claim in strict accordance with the local mining laws of Hurdy-Gurdy, and put up the customary notice.

It is necessary to explain that one of the adjuncts to Hurdy-Gurdy—one to which that metropolis became afterward itself an adjunct—was a cemetery. In the first week of the camp's existence this had been thoughtfully laid out by a committee of citizens. The day after had been signalized by a debate between two members of the committee, with reference to a more eligible site, and on the third day the necropolis was inaugurated by a double funeral. As the camp had waned the cemetery had waxed ; and long before the ultimate inhabitant, victorious alike over the insidious malaria and the forthright revolver, had turned the tail of his pack-ass upon Injun Creek, the outlying settlement had become a populous if not popular suburb. And now, when the town was fallen into the sere and yellow leaf of an unlovely senility, the graveyard—though somewhat marred by time and circumstance, and not altogether exempt from innovations in grammar and experiments in orthography, to say nothing of the devastating coyote— answered the humble needs of its denizens with reasonable completeness. It comprised a generous two acres of ground, which, with commendable thrift but needless care, had been selected for its mineral unworth,

contained two or three skeleton trees (one
of which had a stout lateral branch from
which a weather-wasted rope still significantly dangled), half a hundred gravelly
mounds, a score of rude headboards dis-
playing the literary peculiarities above mentioned, and a struggling colony of prickly
pears. Altogether, God's Location, as with
characteristic reverence it had been called,
could justly boast of an indubitably superior
quality of desolation. It was in the most
thickly settled portion of this interesting
demesne that Mr. Jefferson Doman staked
off his claim. If in the prosecution of his
design he should deem it expedient to remove any of the dead, they would have the
right to be suitably re-interred.

III

This Mr. Jefferson Doman was from Elizabethtown, New Jersey, where, six years
before, he had left his heart in the keeping
of a golden-haired, demure-mannered young
woman named Mary Matthews, as collateral
security for his return to claim her hand.

"I just *know* you'll never get back alive—

you never do succeed in anything,'' was the
remark which illustrated Miss Matthews's
notion of what constituted success, and, in-
ferentially, her view of the nature of encouragement. She added : '' If you don't
I 'll go to California too. I can put the
coins in little bags as you dig them out.''

This characteristically feminine theory of
auriferous deposits did not commend itself to
the masculine intelligence : it was Mr. Doman's belief that gold was found in a liquid
state. He deprecated her intent with considerable enthusiasm, suppressed her sobs with
a light hand upon her mouth, laughed in her
eyes as he kissed away her tears, and, with
a cheerful '' Ta-ta,'' went to California to
labor for her through the long, loveless
years, with a strong heart, an alert hope, and
a steadfast fidelity that never for a moment
forgot what it was about. In the meantime
Miss Matthews had granted a monopoly of
her humble talent for sacking up coins to
Mr. Jo Seeman, of New York, gambler, by
whom it was better appreciated than her
commanding genius for unsacking and be-
stowing them upon his local rivals. Of this
latter aptitude, indeed, he manifested his

disapproval by an act which secured him the
position of clerk of the prison laundry at
Sing Sing, and for her the *sobriquet* of " Split-
faced Moll." At about this time she wrote
to Mr. Doman a touching letter of renuncia-
tion, inclosing her photograph to prove that
she had no longer a right to indulge the
dream of becoming Mrs. Doman, and re-
counting so graphically her fall from a horse
that the staid bronco upon which Mr. Doman had ridden into Red Dog to get the letter, made vicarious atonement under the
spur all the way back to camp. The letter
failed in a signal way to accomplish its object ; the fidelity which had before been to
Mr. Doman a matter of love and duty, was
thenceforth a matter of honor also ; and the
photograph, showing the once pretty face
sadly disfigured as by the slash of a knife,
was duly instated in his affections, and its
more comely predecessor treated with con-
tumelious neglect. On being apprised of
this, Miss Matthews, it is only fair to say,
appeared less surprised than from the apparently low estimate of Mr. Doman's generos-
ity which the tone of her former letter
attested, one would naturally have expected

her to be. Soon after, however, her letters grew infrequent, and then ceased altogether.

But Mr. Doman had another correspondent, Mr. Barney Bree, of Hurdy-Gurdy, formerly of Red Dog. This gentleman, although a notable figure among miners, was not a miner. His knowledge of mining consisted mainly in a marvelous command of its slang, to which he made copious contributions, enriching its vocabulary with a wealth of extraordinary phrases more remarkable for their aptness than their refinement, and which impressed the unlearned "tenderfoot" with a lively sense of the profundity of their inventor's acquirements. When not entertaining a circle of admiring auditors from San Francisco or the East he could commonly be found pursuing the comparatively obscure industry of sweeping out the various dance houses and purifying the spittoons.

Barney had apparently but two passions in life—love of Jefferson Doman, who had once been of some service to him, and love of whisky, which certainly had not. He had been among the first in the rush to Hurdy-Gurdy, but had not prospered, and had sunk by degrees to the position of grave digger. This was not a vocation, but Barney in a desultory way turned his trembling hand to it whenever some local misunderstanding at the card table and his own partial recovery from a prolonged debauch occurred coincidently in point of time. One day Mr. Doman received, at Red Dog, a letter with the simple postmark, "Hurdy, Cal.," and being occupied with another matter, carelessly thrust it into a chink of his cabin for future perusal. Some two years later it was accidentally dislodged, and he read it. It ran as follows:—

"HURDY, June 6.

"FRIEND JEFF: I've hit her hard in the boneyard. She's blind and lousy. I'm on the divvy—that's me, and mum's my lay till you toot.

"Yours,   BARNEY.

"P.S.—I've clayed her with Scarry."

With some knowledge of the general mining camp *argot* and of Mr. Bree's private system for the communication of ideas, Mr. Doman had no difficulty in understanding by this uncommon epistle that Barney, while performing his duty as grave digger, had uncovered a quartz ledge with no outcroppings ; that it was visibly rich in free gold ; that, moved by considerations of friendship, he was willing to accept Mr. Doman as a partner, and pending that gentleman's declaration of his will in the matter would discreetly keep the discovery a secret. From the postscript it was plainly inferable that in order to conceal the treasure he had buried above it the mortal part of a person named Scarry.

From subsequent events, as related to Mr. Doman, at Red Dog, it would appear that before taking this precaution Mr. Bree must have had the thrift to remove a modest competency of the gold ; at any rate, it was at about that time that he entered upon that memorable series of potations and treatings which is still one of the cherished traditions of the San Juan Smith country, and is spoken of with respect as far away as Ghost Rock and Lone Hand. At its conclusion, some former citizens of Hurdy-Gurdy, for whom he had performed the last kindly office at the cemetery, made room for him among them, and he rested well.

IV

Having finished staking off his claim, Mr. Doman walked back to the centre of it and stood again at the spot where his search among the graves had expired in the exclamation, "Scarry." He bent again over the headboard which bore that name, and, as if to reinforce the senses of sight and hearing, ran his forefinger along the rudely carved letters, and, re-erecting himself, appended orally to the simple inscription the shockingly forthright epitaph, "She was a holy terror!"

Had Mr. Doman been required to make these words good with proof—as, considering their somewhat censorious character, he doubtless should have been—he would have found himself embarrassed by the absence of reputable witnesses, and hearsay evidence would have been the best he could command. At the time when Scarry had been prevalent in the mining camps thereabout—when, as the editor of the *Hurdy Herald* would have phrased it, she was "in the plentitude of her power"—Mr. Doman's fortunes had been at a low ebb, and he had led the vagrantly laborious life of a prospector. His time had been mostly spent in the mountains, now with one companion, now with another. It was from the admiring recitals of these casual partners, fresh from the various camps, that his judgment of Scarry had been made up ; he himself had never had the doubtful advantage of her acquaintance and the precarious distinction of her favor. And when, finally, on the termination of her perverse career at Hurdy-Gurdy, he had read in a chance copy of the *Herald* her column-long obituary (written by the local humorist of that lively sheet in the highest style of his art) Doman had paid to her memory and to her historiographer's genius the tribute of a smile, and chivalrously forgotten her. Standing now at the grave-side of this mountain Messalina, he recalled the leading events of her turbulent career, as he had heard them celebrated at his various camp fires, and, perhaps with an unconscious attempt at self-justification, repeated that she was a holy terror, and sank his pick into her grave up to the handle. At that moment a raven, which had silently settled upon a branch of the blasted tree

above his head, solemnly snapped its beak
and uttered its mind about the matter with
an approving croak.

Pursuing his discovery of free gold with
great zeal, which he probably credited to his
conscience as a grave digger, Mr. Barney
Bree had made an unusually deep sepulcher,
and it was near sunset before Mr. Doman,
laboring with the leisurely deliberation of
one who has "a dead sure thing" and no
fear of an adverse claimant's enforcement of
a prior right, reached the coffin and uncovered it. When he had done so, he was confronted by a difficulty for which he had
made no provision ; the coffin—a mere flat
shell of not very well-preserved redwood
boards, apparently—had no handles, and it
filled the entire bottom of the excavation.
The best he could do without violating the
decent sanctities of the situation, was to
make the excavation sufficiently longer to
enable him to stand at the head of the casket,
and, getting his powerful hands underneath,
erect it upon its narrower end ; and this he
proceeded to do. The approach of night
quickened his efforts. He had no thought
of abandoning his task at this stage, to

resume it on the morrow under more advantageous conditions. The feverish stimulation of cupidity and the fascination of terror held him to his dismal work with an iron authority. He no longer idled, but wrought with a terrible zeal. His head uncovered, his upper garments discarded, his shirt opened at the neck, and thrown back from his breast, down which ran sinuous rills of perspiration, this hardy and impenitent gold-getter and grave-robber toiled with a giant energy that almost dignified the character of his horrible purpose ; and when the sun fringes had burned themselves out along the crest line of the western hills, and the full moon had climbed out of the shadows that lay along the purple plain, he had erected the coffin upon its foot, where it stood propped against the end of the open grave. Then, standing up to his neck in the earth at the opposite extreme of the excavation, as he looked at the coffin upon which the moonlight now fell with a full illumination, he was thrilled with a sudden terror to observe upon it the startling apparition of a dark human head—the shadow of his own. For a moment this simple and natural circumstance un-

nerved him. The noise of his labored breathing frightened him, and he tried to still it,
but his bursting lungs would not be denied.
Then, laughing half audibly and wholly
without spirit, he began making movements
of his head from side to side, in order to com-
pel the apparition to repeat them. He found
a comforting reassurance in asserting his
command over his own shadow. He was
temporizing, making, with unconscious pru-
dence, a dilatory opposition to an impending
catastrophe. He felt that invisible forces
of evil were closing in upon him, and he
parleyed for time with the Inevitable.

He now observed in succession several
extraordinary circumstances. The surface
of the coffin upon which his eyes were fastened was not flat ; it presented two distinct
ridges, one longitudinal and the other trans-
verse. Where these intersected at the
widest part, there was a corroded metallic
plate that reflected the moonlight with a
dismal luster. Along the outer edges of the
coffin, at long intervals, were rust-eaten
heads of nails. This frail product of the
carpenter's art had been put into the grave
the wrong side up !

Perhaps it was one of the humors of the
camp—a practical manifestation of the facetious spirit that had found literary expression
in the topsy-turvy obituary notice from the
pen of Hurdy-Gurdy's great humorist. Perhaps it had some occult personal signification
impenetrable to understandings uninstructed
in local traditions. A more charitable hypothesis is that it was owing to a misad-
venture on the part of Mr. Barney Bree,
who, making the interment unassisted (either
by choice for the conservation of his golden
secret, or through public apathy), had committed a blunder which he was afterward
unable or unconcerned to rectify. However
it had come about, poor Scarry had indubitably been put into the earth face downward.

When terror and absurdity make alliance.
the effect is frightful. This strong-hearted
and daring man, this hardy night worker
among the dead, this defiant antagonist of
darkness and desolation, succumbed to a
ridiculous surprise. He was smitten with a
thrilling chill—shivered, and shook his massive shoulders as if to throw off an icy hand.
He no longer breathed, and the blood in his
veins, unable to abate its impetus, surged

hotly beneath his cold skin. Unleavened
with oxygen, it mounted to his head and
congested his brain. His physical functions
had gone over to the enemy ; his very heart
was arrayed against him. He did not move ;
he could not have cried out. He needed but
a coffin to be dead—as dead as the death
that confronted him with only the length of
an open grave and the thickness of a rotting
plank between.

Then, one by one, his senses returned ;
the tide of terror that had overwhelmed his
faculties began to recede. But with the return of his senses he became singularly unconscious of the object of his fear. He saw
the moonlight gilding the coffin, but no longer the coffin that it gilded. Raising his
eyes and turning his head, he noted, curiously and with surprise, the black branches
of the dead tree, and tried to estimate the
length of the weather-worn rope that dangled from its ghostly hand. The monotonous barking of distant coyotes affected him
as something he had heard years ago in a
dream. An owl flapped awkwardly above
him on noiseless wings, and he tried to fore-
cast the direction of its flight when it should

encounter the cliff that reared its illuminated
front a mile away. His hearing took account
of a gopher's stealthy tread in the shadow
of the cactus. He was intensely observant ;
his senses were all alert; but he saw not
the coffin. As one can gaze at the sun until
it looks black and then vanishes, so his
mind, having exhausted its capacities of
dread, was no longer conscious of the separate existence of anything dreadful. The
Assassin was cloaking the sword.

It was during this lull in the battle that
he became sensible of a faint, sickening odor.
At first he thought it was that of a rattle-
snake, and involuntarily tried to look about
his feet. They were nearly invisible in the
gloom of the grave. A hoarse, gurgling
sound, like the death-rattle in a human
throat, seemed to come out of the sky, and
a moment later a great, black, angular
shadow, like the same sound made visible,
dropped curving from the topmost branch
of the spectral tree, fluttered for an instant
before his face, and sailed fiercely away into
the mist along the creek. It was a raven.
The incident recalled him to a sense of the
situation, and again his eyes sought the up-

right coffin, now illuminated by the moon
for half its length.   He saw the gleam of
the metallic plate, and tried without moving
to decipher the inscription.   Then he fell to
speculating upon what was behind it.   His
creative imagination presented him a vivid
picture.   The planks no longer seemed an
obstacle to his vision, and he saw the livid
corpse of the dead woman, standing in grave-
clothes, and staring vacantly at him, with
lidless, shrunken eyes.   The lower jaw
was fallen, the upper lip drawn away from
the uncovered teeth.   He could make out
a mottled pattern on the hollow cheeks—
the maculations of decay   By some mysterious process, his mind reverted for the
first time that day to the photograph of
Mary Matthews.   He contrasted its blonde
beauty with the forbidding aspect of this
dead face—the most beloved object that he
knew with the most hideous that he could
conceive.

The Assassin now advanced, and, display-
ing the blade, laid it against the victim's
throat.   That is to say, the man became at
first dimly, then definitely, aware of an impressive coincidence—a relation—a parallel,

between the face on the card and the name on the headboard. The one was disfigured, the other described a disfiguration. The thought took hold of him and shook him. It transformed the face that his imagination had created behind the coffin lid ; the contrast became a resemblance ; the resemblance grew to identity. Remembering the many descriptions of Scarry's personal appearance that he had heard from the gossips of his camp fire, he tried with imperfect success to recall the exact nature of the disfiguration that had given the woman her ugly name ; and what was lacking in his memory, fancy supplied, stamping it with the validity of conviction. In the maddening attempt to recall such scraps of the woman's history as he had heard, the muscles of his arms and hands were strained to a painful tension, as by an effort to lift a great weight. His body writhed and twisted with the exertion. The tendons of his neck stood out as tense as whip corps, and his breath came in short, sharp gasps. The catastrophe could not be much longer delayed, or the agony of antici-pation would leave nothing to be done by the *coup de grâce* of verification. The scarred face behind the coffin lid would slay him through the wood.

A movement of the coffin calmed him. It came forward to within a foot of his face, growing visibly larger as it approached. The rusted metallic plate, with an inscription illegible in the moonlight, looked him steadily in the eye. Determined not to shrink, he tried to brace his shoulders more firmly against the end of the excavation, and nearly fell backward in the attempt. There was nothing to support him ; he had moved upon his enemy, clutching the heavy knife that he had drawn from his belt. The coffin had not advanced, and he smiled to think it could not retreat. Lifting his knife, he struck the heavy hilt against the metal plate with all his power. There was a sharp, ringing percussion, and with a dull clatter the whole decayed coffin lid broke in pieces and came away, falling about his feet. The quick and the dead were face to face—the frenzied, shrieking man—the woman standing tranquil in her silences. She was a holy terror !

V

Some months later a party of men and women belonging to the highest social circles of San Francisco passed through Hurdy-Gurdy on their way to the Yosemite Valley by a new trail. They halted for dinner, and, during its preparation, explored the desolate camp. One of the party had been at Hurdy-Gurdy in the days of its glory. He had, indeed, been one of its prominent citizens; and it used to be said that more money passed over his faro table in any one night than over those of all his competitors in a week; but being now a millionaire engaged in greater enterprises, he did not deem these early successes of sufficient importance to merit the distinction of remark. His invalid wife, a lady famous in San Francisco for the costly nature of her entertainments and her exacting rigor with regard to the social position and antecedents of those who attended them, accompanied the expedition. During a stroll among the shanties of the abandoned camp, Mr. Porfer directed the attention of his wife and friends to a dead tree on a low hill beyond Injun Creek.

"As I told you," he said, "I passed through this camp in 1852, and was told that no fewer than five men had been hanged here by vigilantes at various times, and all on that tree. If I am not mistaken, a rope is dangling from it yet. Let us go over and see the place."

Mr. Porfer did not add that the rope in question was perhaps the very one from whose fatal embrace his own neck had once had an escape so narrow that an hour's delay in taking himself out of that region would have spanned it.

Proceedingly leisurely down the creek to a convenient crossing, the party came upon the cleanly-picked skeleton of an animal, which Mr. Porfer, after due examination, pronounced to be that of an ass. The distinguishing ears were gone, but much of the inedible head had been spared by the beasts and birds, and the stout bridle of horsehair was intact, as was the riata, of similar material, connecting it with a picket pin still firmly sunken in the earth. The wooden and metallic elements of a miner's kit lay near by. The customary remarks were made, cynical on the part of the men, sentimental and refined by the lady. A little later they stood by the tree in the cemetery, and Mr. Porfer sufficiently unbent from his dignity to place himself beneath the rotten rope and confidently lay a coil of it about his neck, somewhat, it appeared, to his own satisfaction, but greatly to the horror of his wife, to whose sensibilities the performance gave a smart shock.

An exclamation from one of the party gathered them all about an open grave, at the bottom of which they saw a confused mass of human bones, and the broken remnants of a coffin. Wolves and buzzards had performed the last sad rites for pretty much all else. Two skulls were visible and, in order to investigate this somewhat unusual redundancy one of the younger men had the hardihood to spring into the grave and hand them up to another before Mrs. Porfer could indicate her marked disapproval of so shocking an act, which, nevertheless, she did with considerable feeling and in very choice words. Pursuing his search among the dismal débris at the bottom of the grave, the young man next handed up a rusted coffin plate, with a rudely-cut inscription, which,

with difficulty, Mr. Porfer deciphered and
read aloud with an earnest and not altogether
unsuccessful attempt at the dramatic effect
which he deemed befitting to the occasion
and his rhetorical abilities :

" MANUELITA MURPHY.
Born at the Mission San Pedro—Died in
Hurdy-Gurdy,
Aged 47.
Hell 's full of such."

In deference to the piety of the reader and
the nerves of Mrs. Porfer's fastidious sister-
hood of both sexes let us not touch upon
the painful impression produced by this uncommon inscription, further than to say that
the elocutionary powers of Mr. Porfer had
never before met with so spontaneous and
overwhelming recognition.

The next morsel that rewarded the ghoul
in the grave was a long tangle of black hair,
defiled with clay : but this was such an anti-
climax that it received little attention.
Suddenly, with a short exclamation and a
gesture of excitement, the young man un-
earthed a fragment of grayish rock, and
after a hurried inspection handed it up to
Mr. Porfer.   As the sunlight fell upon it, it

glittered with a yellow luster—it was thickly studded with gleaming points. Mr. Porfer snatched it, bent his head over it a moment, and threw it lightly away, with the simple remark :—

" Iron pyrites—fool's gold."

The young man in the discovery shaft was a trifle disconcerted, apparently.

Meanwhile Mrs. Porfer, unable longer to endure the disagreeable business, had walked back to the tree and seated herself at its root. While rearranging a tress of golden hair, which had slipped from its confinement, she was attracted by what appeared to be, and really was, the fragment of an old coat. Looking about to assure herself that so unladylike an act was not observed, she thrust her jeweled hand into the exposed breast pocket, and drew out a moldy pocket-book. Its contents were as follows :—

One bundle of letters, postmarked Elizabethtown, New Jersey.

One circle of blonde hair tied with a ribbon.

One photograph of a beautiful girl.

One ditto of same singularly disfigured.

One name on back of photograph—'' Jefferson Doman.''

A few moments later a group of anxious
gentlemen surrounded Mrs. Porfer as she
sat motionless at the foot of the tree, her
head dropped forward, her fingers clutching a crushed photograph. Her husband
raised her head, exposing a face ghastly
white, except the long, deforming cicatrice,
familiar to all her friends, which no art could
ever hide, and which now traversed the
pallor of her countenance like a visible
curse.

Mary Matthews Porfer had the bad luck
to be dead.

The Suitable Surroundings

THE NIGHT

ONE midsummer night a farmer's boy living about ten miles from the city of Cincinnati was following a bridle path through a dense and dark forest. He had been searching for some missing cows, and at nightfall found himself a long way from home, and in a part of the country with which he was but partly familiar. But he was a stout-hearted lad, and knowing his general direction from his home, he plunged into the forest without hesitation, guided by the stars. Coming into the bridle path, and observing that it ran in the right direction, he followed it.

The night was clear, but in the woods it was exceedingly dark. It was more by the

sense of touch than by that of sight that the
lad kept the path. He could not, indeed,
very easily go astray ; the undergrowth on
both sides was so thick as to be almost impenetrable. He had gone into the forest a
mile or more when he was surprised to see a
feeble gleam of light shining through the
foliage skirting the path on his left. The
sight of it startled him, and set his heart
beating audibly.

" The old Breede house is somewhere
about here," he said to himself. " This
must be the other end of the path which we
reach it by from our side. Ugh ! what
should a light be doing there ? I don't like
it."

Nevertheless, he pushed on. A moment
later he had emerged from the forest into a
small, open space, mostly upgrown to brambles. There were remnants of a rotting
fence. A few yards from the trail, in the
middle of the " clearing," was the house,
from which the light came through an unglazed window. The window had once contained glass, but that and its supporting
frame had long ago yielded to missiles flung
by hands of venturesome boys, to attest

alike their courage and their hostility to the supernatural ; for the Breede house bore the evil reputation of being haunted. Possibly it was not, but even the hardiest skeptic could not deny that it was deserted—which, in rural regions, is much the same thing.

Looking at the mysterious dim light shining from the ruined window, the boy remembered with apprehension that his own hand had assisted at the destruction. His penitence was, of course, poignant in proportion to its tardiness and inefficacy. He half expected to be set upon by all the unworldly and bodiless malevolences whom he had outraged by assisting to break alike their windows and their peace. Yet this stubborn lad, shaking in every limb, would not retreat. The blood in his veins was strong and rich with the iron of the frontiersman. He was but two removes from the generation which had subdued the Indian. He started to pass the house.

As he was going by, he looked in at the blank window space, and saw a strange and terrifying sight,—the figure of a man seated in the centre of the room, at a table upon which lay some loose sheets of paper. The elbows rested on the table, the hands supporting the head, which was uncovered. On each side the fingers were pushed into the hair. The face showed dead-yellow in the light of a single candle a little to one side. The flame illuminated that side of the face, the other was in deep shadow. The man's eyes were fixed upon the blank window space with a stare in which an older and cooler observer might have discerned something of apprehension, but which seemed to the lad altogether soulless. He believed the man to be dead.

The situation was horrible, but not without its fascination. The boy paused in his flight to note it all. He endeavored to still the beating of his heart by holding his breath until half suffocated. He was weak, faint, trembling ; he could feel the blood forsaking his face. Nevertheless, he set his teeth and resolutely advanced to the house. He had no conscious intention—it was the mere courage of terror. He thrust his white face forward into the illuminated opening. At that instant a strange, harsh cry, a shriek, broke upon the silence of the night,—the note of a screech owl. The man sprang to his feet, overturning the table and extinguishing the candle. The boy took to his heels.

THE DAY BEFORE

"Good-morning, Colston. I am in luck, it seems. You have often said that my commendation of your literary work was mere civility, and here you find me absorbed—actually merged—in your latest story in the *Messenger.* Nothing less shocking than your touch upon my shoulder would have roused me to consciousness."

"The proof is stronger than you seem to know," replied the man addressed; "so keen is your eagerness to read my story that you are willing to renounce selfish considerations and forego all the pleasure that you could get from it."

"I don't understand you," said the other, folding the newspaper that he held, and putting it in his pocket. "You writers are a queer lot, anyhow. Come, tell me what I have done or omitted in this matter. In what way does the pleasure that I get, or might get, from your work depend on me?"

"In many ways. Let me ask you how you would enjoy your breakfast if you took it in this street car. Suppose the phonograph so perfected as to be able to give you an entire opera,—singing, orchestration, and all; do you think you would get much pleasure out of it if you turned it on at your office during business hours? Do you really care for a serenade by Schubert when you hear it fiddled by an untimely Italian on a morning ferryboat? Are you always cocked and primed for admiration? Do you keep every mood on tap, ready to any demand? Let me remind you, sir, that the story which you have done me the honor to begin as a means of becoming oblivious to the discomfort of this car is a ghost story!"

"Well?"

"Well! Has the reader no duties corresponding to his privileges? You have paid five cents for that newspaper. It is yours. You have the right to read it when and where you will. Much of what is in it is neither helped nor harmed by time, and place, and mood; some of it actually requires to be read at once—while it is fizzing. But my story is not of that character. It is

not the 'very latest advices' from Ghost-
land. You are not expected to keep yourself *au courant* with what is going on in the
realm of spooks. The stuff will keep until
you have leisure to put yourself into the
frame of mind appropriate to the sentiment
of the piece—which I respectfully submit
that you cannot do in a street car, even if
you are the only passenger. The solitude is
not of the right sort. An author has rights
which the reader is bound to respect."

"For specific example?"

"The right to the reader's undivided attention. To deny him this is immoral. To
make him share your attention with the rattle of a street car, the moving panorama of
the crowds on the sidewalks, and the buildings beyond—with any of the thousands of
distractions which make our customary environment—is to treat him with gross in-
justice. By God, it is infamous!"

The speaker had risen to his feet, and was
steadying himself by one of the straps hanging from the roof of the car. The other man
looked up at him in sudden astonishment,
wondering how so trivial a grievance could
seem to justify so strong language. He

saw that his friend's face was uncommonly
pale, and that his eyes glowed like living
coals.

"You know what I mean," continued the
writer, impetuously, crowding his words—
"You know what I mean, Marsh. My stuff
in this morning's *Messenger* is plainly sub-
headed 'A Ghost Story.' That is ample
notice to all. Every honorable reader will
understand it as prescribing by implication
the conditions under which the work is to be
read."

The man addressed as Marsh winced a trifle, then asked with a smile : "What conditions? You know that I am only a plain
business man, who cannot be supposed to
understand such things. How, when, where
should I read your ghost story ? "

"In solitude—at night—by the light of a
candle. There are certain emotions which a
writer can easily enough excite—such as
compassion or merriment. I can move you
to tears or laughter under almost any circumstances. But for my ghost story to be effective you must be made to feel fear—at least
a strong sense of the supernatural—and that
is a different matter. I have a right to ex-

pect that if you read me at all you will give
me a chance ; that you will make yourself
accessible to the emotion that I try to in-
spire."

The car had now arrived at its terminus
and stopped.   The trip just completed was
its first for the day, and the conversation of
the two early passengers had not been interrupted.   The streets were yet silent and
desolate ; the house tops were just touched
by the rising sun.   As they stepped from
the car and walked away together Marsh
narrowly eyed his companion, who was reported, like most men of uncommon literary
ability, to be addicted to various destructive
vices.   That is the revenge which dull
minds take upon bright ones in resentment
of their superiority.   Mr. Colston was
known as a man of genius.   There are honest souls who believe that genius is a mode
of excess.   It was known that Colston did
not drink liquor, but many said that he ate
opium.   Something in his appearance that
morning—a certain wildness of the eyes, an
unusual pallor, a thickness and rapidity of
speech—were taken by Mr. Marsh to confirm
the report.   Nevertheless, he had not the

self-denial to abandon a subject which he found interesting, however it might excite his friend.

"Do you mean to say," he began, "that if I take the trouble to observe your directions—place myself in the condition which you demand : solitude, night and a tallow candle—you can with your ghastliest work give me an uncomfortable sense of the supernatural, as you call it ? Can you accelerate my pulse, make me start at sudden noises, send a nervous chill along my spine, and cause my hair to rise ? "

Colston turned suddenly and looked him squarely in the eyes as they walked. "You would not dare—you have not the courage," he said. He emphasized the words with a contemptuous gesture. "You are brave enough to read me in a street car, but—in a deserted house—alone—in the forest—at night ! Bah ! I have a manuscript in my pocket that would kill you."

Marsh was angry. He knew himself courageous, and the words stung him. "If you know such a place," he said, " take me there to-night and leave me your story and a candle. Call for me when I've had time enough to read it, and I'll tell you the entire plot and—kick you out of the place.''

That is how it occurred that the farmer's boy, looking in at an unglazed window of the Breede house, saw a man sitting in the light of a candle.

THE DAY AFTER

Late in the afternoon of the next day three men and a boy approached the Breede house from that point of the compass toward which the boy had fled the preceding night. They were in high spirits apparently ; they talked loudly and laughed. They made facetious and good-humored ironical remarks to the boy about his adventure, which evidently they did not believe in. The boy accepted their raillery with seriousness, making no reply. He had a sense of the fitness of things, and knew that one who professes to have seen a dead man rise from his seat and blow out a candle is not a credible witness.

Arrived at the house, and finding the door bolted on the inside, the party of investigators entered without further ceremony than breaking it down. Leading out of the passage into which this door had opened was another on the right and one on the left. These two doors also were fastened, and were broken in. They entered at random the one on the left first. It was vacant. In the room on the right—the one which had the blank front window—was the dead body of a man.

It lay partly on one side, with the forearm beneath it, the cheek on the floor. The eyes were wide open ; the stare was not an agreeable thing to encounter. The lower jaw had fallen ; a little pool of saliva had collected beneath the mouth. An overthrown table, a partly-burned candle, a chair, and some paper with writing on it, were all else that the room contained. The men looked at the body, touching the face in turn. The boy gravely stood at the head, assuming a look of ownership. It was the proudest moment of his life. One of the men said to him, " You 're a good 'un "—a remark which was received by the two others with nods of acquiescence. It was Skepticism apologizing to Truth. Then one of the men took from the floor the sheet of manuscript and stepped to the window, for already the eve-

ning shadows were glooming the forest. The
song of the whip-poor-will was heard in the
distance, and a monstrous beetle sped by the
window on roaring wings, and thundered
away out of hearing.

THE MANUSCRIPT

" Before committing the act which, rightly
or wrongly, I have resolved on, and appearing before my Maker for judgment, I, James
R. Colston, deem it my duty as a journalist to
make a statement to the public. My name
is, I believe, tolerably well known to the people as a writer of tragic tales, but the somber-
est imagination never conceived anything
so gloomy as my own life and history. Not
in incident : my life has been destitute of
adventure and action. But my mental career
has been lurid with experiences such as kill
and damn. I shall not recount them here—
some of them are written and ready for publi-
cation elsewhere. The object of these lines is
to explain to whomsoever may be interested
that my death is voluntary—my own act. I
shall die at twelve o'clock on the night of
the 15th of July—a significant anniversary to

me, for it was on that day, and at that hour, that my friend in time and eternity, Charles Breede, performed his vow to me by the same act which his fidelity to our pledge now entails upon me. He took his life in his little house in the Copeton woods. There was the customary verdict of 'temporary insanity.' Had I testified at that inquest—had I told all I knew, they would have called *me* mad !

"I have still a week of life in which to arrange my worldly affairs, and prepare for the great change. It is enough, for I have but few affairs, and it is now four years since death became an imperative obligation.

"I shall bear this writing on my body; the finder will please hand it to the coroner.

"JAMES R. COLSTON.

"P. S.—Willard Marsh, on this the fatal fifteenth day of July, I hand you this manuscript, to be opened and read under the conditions agreed upon, and at the place which I designated. I forego my intention to keep it on my body to explain the manner of my death, which is not important. It will serve to explain the manner of yours. I am to call for you during the night to receive assurance that you have read the manuscript. You know me well enough to expect me. But, my friend, it *will be after twelve o'clock.* May God have mercy on our souls!"

"J. R. C."

Before the man who was reading this manuscript had finished, the candle had been picked up and lighted. When the reader had done, he quietly thrust the paper against the flame, and despite the protestations of the others held it until it was burnt to ashes. The man who did this, and who afterward placidly endured a severe reprimand from the coroner, was a son-in-law of the late Charles Breede. At the inquest nothing could elicit an intelligible account of what the paper had contained.

FROM "THE TIMES"

"Yesterday the Commissioners of Lunacy committed to the asylum Mr. James R. Colston, a writer of some local reputation, connected with the *Messenger.* It will be remembered that on the evening of the 15th inst. Mr. Colston was given into custody by one of his fellow-lodgers in the Baine House, who had observed him acting very suspiciously, baring his throat and whetting a razor—occasionally trying its edge by actually cutting through the skin of his arm, etc. On being handed over to the police, the unfortunate man made a desperate resistance and has ever since been so violent that it has been necessary to keep him in a straitjacket. Most of our esteemed contemporary's other writers are still at large."

An Inhabitant of Carcosa

For there be divers sorts of death—some wherein the body remaineth ; and in some it vanisheth quite away with the spirit. This commonly occureth only in solitude (such is God's will) and, none seeing the end, we say the man is lost, or gone on a long journey—which indeed he hath ; but sometimes it hath happened in sight of many, as abundant testimony showeth. In one kind of death the spirit also dieth, and this it hath been known to do while yet the body was in vigor for many years. Sometimes, as is veritably attested, it dieth with the body but after a season it is raised up again in that place that the body did decay.

PONDERING these words of Hali (whom God rest) and questioning their full meaning, as one who, having an intimation yet doubts if there be not something behind other than that which he has discerned, I noted not whither I had strayed until a sud-

den chill wind striking my face revived in
me a sense of my surroundings. I observed
with astonishment that everything seemed
unfamiliar. On every side of me stretched
a bleak and desolate expanse of plain, covered with a tall overgrowth of sere grass,
which rustled and whistled in the autumn
wind with heaven knows what mysterious
and disquieting suggestion. Protruded at
long intervals above it, stood strangely-
shaped and somber-colored rocks, which
seemed to have an understanding with one
another and to exchange looks of uncomfortable significance, as if they had reared their
heads to watch the issue of some foreseen
event. A few blasted trees here and there
appeared as leaders in this malevolent conspiracy of silent expectation. The day, I
thought, must be far advanced, though the
sun was invisible ; and although sensible
that the air was raw and chill, my consciousness of that fact was rather mental than
physical—I had no feeling of discomfort.
Over all the dismal landscape a canopy of
low, lead-colored clouds hung like a visible
curse. In all there were a menace and a
portent—a hint of crime, an intimation of

doom.   Bird, beast, or insect there was
none.   The wind sighed in the bare branches
of the dead trees and the gray grass bent to
whisper its dead secret to the earth ; but
no other sound or motion broke the awful
repose of that dismal place.

I observed in the herbage a number of
weather-worn stones, evidently shaped with
tools.   They were broken, covered with
moss and half sunken in the earth.   Some
lay prostrate, some leaned at various angles,
none was vertical.   They were obviously
headstones of graves, though the graves
themselves no longer existed as either
mounds or depressions ; the years had level-
led all.   Scattered here and there, more
massive blocks showed where some pompous
tomb or ambitious monument had once flung
its feeble defiance at oblivion.   So old
seemed these relics, these vestiges of vanity
and memorials of affection and piety—so
battered and worn and stained—so neglected,
deserted, forgotten the place, that I could
not help thinking myself the discoverer of
the burial-ground of a prehistoric race of
men—a nation whose very name was long
extinct.

Filled with these reflections, I was for some time heedless of the sequence of my own experiences, but soon I thought, " How came I hither?" A moment's reflection seemed to make this all clear, and explain at the same time, though in a disquieting way, the singular character with which my fancy had invested all that I saw and heard. I was ill. I remembered now that I had been prostrated by a sudden fever, and that my family had told me that in my periods of delirium I had constantly cried out for liberty and air, and had been held in bed to prevent my escape out-of-doors. Now I had eluded the vigilance of my attendants, and had wandered hither to—to where? I could not conjecture. Clearly I was at a considerable distance from the city where I dwelt—the ancient and famous city of Carcosa. No signs of human life were anywhere visible or audible ; no rising smoke, no watchdog's bark, no lowing of cattle, no shouts of children at play—nothing but that dismal burial-place, with its air of mystery and dread, due to my own disordered brain. Was I not becoming again delirious, there, beyond human aid? Was it not indeed *all* an illusion of my madness? I called aloud the names of my wives and sons, reached out my hands in search of theirs, even as I walked among the crumbling stones and in the withered grass.

A noise behind me caused me to turn about. A wild animal—a lynx—was approaching. The thought came to me : If I break down here in the desert—if the fever returns and I fail, this beast will be at my throat. I sprang toward it, shouting. It trotted tranquilly by, within a hand's breadth of me, and disappeared behind a rock. A moment later a man's head appeared to rise out of the ground a short distance away. He was ascending the farther slope of a low hill whose crest was hardly to be distinguished from the general level. His whole figure soon came into view against the background of gray cloud. He was half naked, half clad in skins. His hair was unkempt, his beard long and ragged. In one hand he carried a bow and arrow ; the other held a blazing torch with a long trail of black smoke. He walked slowly and with caution, as if he feared falling into some open grave concealed by

the tall grass. This strange apparition
surprised but did not alarm, and, taking
such a course as to intercept him, I met him
almost face to face, accosting him with the
salutation, " God keep you ! "

He gave no heed, nor did he arrest his
pace.

" Good stranger," I continued, " I am ill
and lost.   Direct me, I beseech you, to Carcosa ? "

The man broke into a barbarous chant in
an unknown tongue, passing on and away.
An owl on the branch of a decayed tree
hooted dismally, and was answered by
another in the distance.   Looking upward I
saw, through a sudden rift in the clouds,
Aldebaran and the Hyades !   In all this
there was a hint of night—the lynx, the
man with a torch, the owl.   Yet I saw—I
saw even the stars in absence of the darkness.
I saw, but was apparently not seen nor
heard.   Under what awful spell did I exist?

I seated myself at the root of a great tree,
seriously to consider what it was best to do.
That I was mad I could no longer doubt,
yet recognized a ground of doubt in the
conviction.   Of fever I had no trace.   I had,

withal, a sense of exhilaration and vigor altogether unknown to me—a feeling of mental and physical exaltation. My senses seemed all alert; I could feel the air as a ponderous substance, I could hear the silence.

A great root of the giant tree against whose trunk I leaned as I sat, held inclosed in its grasp a slab of stone, a part of which protruded into a recess formed by another root. The stone was thus partly protected from the weather, though greatly decomposed. Its edges were worn round, its corners eaten away, its face deeply furrowed and scaled. Glittering particles of mica were visible in the earth about it—vestiges of its decomposition. This stone had apparently marked the grave out of which the tree had sprung ages ago. The tree's exacting roots had robbed the grave and made the stone a prisoner.

A sudden wind pushed some dry leaves and twigs from the uppermost face of the stone; I saw the low-relief letters of an inscription and bent to read it. God in Heaven! *my* name in full!—the date of *my* birth!—the date of *my* death!

A level shaft of rosy light illuminated the whole side of the tree as I sprang to my feet in terror. The sun was rising in the east. I stood between the tree and his broad red disk—no shadow darkened the trunk !

A chorus of howling wolves saluted the dawn. I saw them sitting on their haunches, singly and in groups, on the summits of irregular mounds and tumuli, filling a half of my desert prospect and extending to the horizon ; and then I knew that these were ruins of the ancient and famous city of Carcosa.

Such are the facts imparted to the medium Bayrolles by the spirit Hoseib Alar Robardin.

The Boarded Window

IN 1830, only a few miles away from what is now the great city of Cincinnati, lay an immense and almost unbroken forest. The whole region was sparsely settled by people of the frontier—restless souls who no sooner had hewn fairly habitable homes out of the wilderness and attained to that degree of prosperity which to-day we should call indigence than, impelled by some mysterious impulse of their nature, they abandoned all and pushed further westward, to encounter new perils and privations in the effort to regain the meagre comforts which they had voluntarily renounced. Many of them had already forsaken that region for the remoter settlements, but among those remaining was one who had been of those first arriving. He lived alone in a house of logs, surrounded

on all sides by the great forest, of whose
gloom and silence he seemed a part, for no
one had ever known him to smile or speak
a needless word. His simple wants were
supplied by the sale or barter of skins of
wild animals in the river town, for not a
thing did he grow upon the land which he
might, if needful, have claimed by right of
undisturbed possession. There were evidences of "improvement"—a few acres of
ground immediately about the house had
once been cleared of its trees, the decayed
stumps of which were half concealed by the
new growth that had been suffered to repair
the ravage wrought by the ax at some distant day. Apparently the man's zeal for
agriculture had burned with a failing flame,
expiring in penitential ashes.

The little log house, with its chimney of
sticks, its roof of warping clapboards
weighted with traversing poles and its
"chinking" of clay, had a single door,
and, directly opposite, a window. The latter, however, was boarded up—nobody could
remember a time when it was not. And
none knew why it was so closed; certainly
not because of the occupant's dislike of

light and air, for on those rare occasions when a hunter had passed that lonely spot, the recluse had commonly been seen sunning himself on his doorstep if heaven had provided sunshine for his need. I fancy there are few persons living to-day who ever knew the secret of that window, but I am one, as you shall see.

The man's name was said to be Murlock. He was apparently seventy years old, actually about fifty. Something besides years had had a hand in his aging. His hair and long, full beard were white, his gray, lustreless eyes sunken, his face singularly seamed with wrinkles, which appeared to belong to two intersecting systems. In figure he was tall and spare, with a stoop of the shoulders —a burden bearer. I never saw him ; these particulars I learned from my grandfather, from whom also I got the story when I was a lad. He had known him when living near by in that early day.

One day Murlock was found in his cabin, dead. It was not a time and place for coroners and newspapers, and I suppose it was agreed that he had died from natural causes or I should have been told, and should remember. I only know that, with what was probably a sense of the fitness of things, the body was buried near the cabin, alongside the grave of his wife, who had preceded him by so many years that local tradition had retained hardly a hint of her existence. That closes the final chapter of this true story—excepting, indeed, the circumstance that many years afterward, in company with an equally intrepid spirit, I penetrated to the place and ventured near enough to the ruined cabin to throw a stone against it, and ran away to avoid the ghost which every well-informed boy thereabout knew haunted the spot. But there is an earlier chapter—that supplied by my grandfather.

When Murlock built his cabin and began laying sturdily about with his ax to hew out a farm—the rifle, meanwhile, his means of support—he was young, strong, and full of hope. In that eastern country whence he came he had married, as was the fashion, a young woman in all ways worthy of his honest devotion, who shared the dangers and privations of his lot with a willing spirit and light heart. There is no known record of her name; of her charms of mind and per-

son tradition is silent and the doubter is at
liberty to entertain his doubt ; but God forbid that I should share it ! Of their affection
and happiness there is abundant assurance
in every added day of the man's widowed
life ; for what but the magnetism of a blessed
memory could have chained that venturesome spirit to a lot like that?

One day Murlock returned from gunning
in a distant part of the forest to find his wife
prostrate with fever and delirious. There
was no physician within miles, no neighbor,
nor was she in a condition to be left, to sum-
mon help. So he set about the task of nurs-
ing her back to health, but at the end of the
third day she fell into unconsciousness and
so passed away, apparently, with never a
gleam of returning reason.

From what we know of a nature like his
we may venture to sketch in some of the details of the outline picture drawn by my
grandfather. When convinced that she was
dead, Murlock had sense enough to remember that the dead must be prepared for burial. In performance of this sacred duty he
blundered now and again, did certain things
incorrectly, and others which he did correctly

were done over and over. His occasional
failures to accomplish some simple and ordinary act filled him with astonishment, like
that of a drunken man who wonders at the
suspension of familiar natural laws. He was
surprised, too, that he did not weep—surprised and a little ashamed ; surely it is
unkind not to weep for the dead. " To-morrow," he said aloud, " I shall have to make
the coffin and dig the grave ; and then I
shall miss her, when she is no longer in
sight, but now—she is dead, of course, but
it is all right—it *must* be all right, somehow.
Things cannot be as bad as they seem."

He stood over the body in the fading light,
adjusting the hair and putting the finishing
touches to the simple toilet, doing all mechanically, with soulless care. And still
through his consciousness ran an undersense
of conviction that all was right—that he
should have her again as before, and everything explained. He had had no experience in grief ; his capacity had not been
enlarged by use. His heart could not con-
tain it all, nor his imagination rightly conceive it. He did not know he was so hard
hit ; that knowledge would come later, and

never go. Grief is an artist of powers as various as the instruments upon which he plays his dirges for the dead, evoking from some the sharpest, shrillest notes, from others the low, grave chords that throb recurrent like the slow beating of a distant drum. Some natures it startles ; some it stupefies. To one it comes like the stroke of an arrow, stinging all the sensibilities to a keener life ; to another as the blow of a bludgeon, which in crushing benumbs. We may conceive Murlock to have been that way affected, for (and here we are upon surer ground than that of conjecture) no sooner had he finished his pious work than, sinking into a chair by the side of the table upon which the body lay, and noting how white the profile showed in the deepening gloom, then laying his arms upon the table's edge, he dropped his face into them, tearless yet and unutterably weary. At that moment came in through the open window a long, wailing sound like the cry of a lost child in the far deeps of the darkening wood ! But the man did not move. Again, and nearer than before, sounded that unearthly cry upon his failing sense. Perhaps it was a wild beast ; perhaps it was a dream. For Murlock was asleep.

Some hours later, as it afterward appeared, this unfaithful watcher awoke, and lifting his head from his arms, intently listened—he knew not why. There in the black darkness by the side of the dead, recalling all without a shock, he strained his eyes to see—he knew not what. His senses were all alert, his breath was suspended, his blood had stilled its tides as if to assist the silence. Who—what had waked him, and where was it?

Suddenly the table shook beneath his arms, and at the same moment he heard, or fancied that he heard, a light, soft step—another—sounds as of bare feet upon the floor!

He was terrified beyond the power to cry out or move. Perforce he waited—waited there in the darkness through seeming centuries of such dread as one may know yet live to tell. He tried vainly to speak the dead woman's name, vainly to stretch forth his hand across the table to learn if she were there. His throat was powerless, his arms and hands were like lead. Then occurred something most frightful. Some heavy body seemed hurled against the table with an impetus that pushed it against his breast so sharply as nearly to overthrow him, and at the same instant he heard and felt the fall of something upon the floor with so violent a thump that the whole house was shaken by the impact. A scuffling ensued, and a confusion of sounds impossible to describe. Murlock had risen to his feet. Fear had by excess forfeited control of his faculties. He flung his hands upon the table. Nothing was there !

There is a point at which terror may turn to madness ; and madness incites to action. With no definite intent, from no motive but the wayward impulse of a madman, Murlock sprang to the wall, with a little groping seized his loaded rifle, and without aim discharged it. By the flash which lit up the room with a vivid illumination, he saw an enormous panther dragging the dead woman toward the window, its teeth fixed in her throat ! Then there were darkness blacker than before, and silence ; and when he returned to consciousness the sun was high and the wood vocal with songs of birds.

The body lay near the window, where the beast had left it when frightened away by the flash and report of the rifle. The clothing was deranged, the long hair in disorder, the limbs lay anyhow. From the throat, dreadfully lacerated, had issued a pool of blood not yet entirely coagulated. The ribbon with which he had bound the wrists was broken ; the hands were tightly clenched. Between the teeth was a fragment of the animal's ear.

The Middle Toe of the Right Foot

I

IT is well known that the old Manton house is haunted. In all the rural district near about, and even in the town of Marshall, a mile away, not one person of unbiased mind entertains a doubt of it; incredulity is confined to those opinionated people who will be called "cranks" as soon as the useful word shall have penetrated the intellectual demesne of the Marshall *Advance*. The evidence that the house is haunted is of two kinds: the testimony of disinterested witnesses who have had ocular proof, and that of the house itself. The former may be disregarded and ruled out on any of the various grounds of objection which may be urged against it by the ingenious ; but facts within the observation of all are material and controlling.

In the first place, the Manton house has been unoccupied by mortals for more than ten years, and with its outbuildings is slowly falling into decay—a circumstance which in itself the judicious will hardly venture to ignore. It stands a little way off the loneliest reach of the Marshall and Harriston road, in an opening which was once a farm and is still disfigured with strips of rotting fence and half covered with brambles overrunning a stony and sterile soil long unacquainted with the plow. The house itself is in tolerably good condition, though badly weather-stained and in dire need of attention from the glazier, the smaller male population of the region having attested in the manner of its kind its disapproval of dwellings without dwellers. The house is two stories in height, nearly square, its front pierced by a single doorway flanked on each side by a window boarded up to the very top. Corresponding windows above, not protected, serve to admit light and rain to the rooms of the upper floor. Grass and weeds grow pretty rankly all about, and a few shade trees, somewhat the worse for wind and leaning all in one direction, seem to be making a concerted effort to run away. In short, as the Marshall town humorist explained in the columns of the *Advance*, " the proposition that the Manton house is badly haunted is the only logical conclusion from the premises." The fact that in this dwelling Mr. Manton thought it expedient one night some ten years ago to rise and cut the throats of his his wife and two small children, removing at once to another part of the country, has no doubt done its share in directing public attention to the fitness of the place for supernatural phenomena.

To this house, one summer evening, came four men in a wagon. Three of them promptly alighted, and the one who had been driving hitched the team to the only remaining post of what had been a fence. The fourth remained seated in the wagon. " Come," said one of his companions, approaching him, while the others moved away in the direction of the dwelling—" this is the place."

The man addressed was pale and trembled visibly. " By God ! " he said harshly, " this is a trick, and it looks to me as if you were in it."

"Perhaps I am," the other said, looking him straight in the face and speaking in a tone which had something of contempt in it. "You will remember, however, that the choice of place was, with your own assent, left to the other side. Of course if you are afraid of spooks—"

"I am afraid of nothing," the man interrupted with another oath, and sprang to the ground. The two then joined the others at the door, which one of them had already opened with some difficulty, caused by rust of lock and hinge. All entered. Inside it was dark, but the man who had unlocked the door produced a candle and matches and made a light. He then unlocked a door on their right as they stood in the passage. This gave them entrance to a large, square room, which the candle but dimly lighted. The floor had a thick carpeting of dust, which partly muffled their footfalls. Cobwebs were in the angles of the walls and depended from the ceiling like strips of rotting lace, making undulatory movements in the disturbed air. The room had two

windows in adjoining sides, but from neither
could anything be seen except the rough
inner surfaces of boards a few inches from
the glass. There was no fireplace, no furniture ; there was nothing. Besides the
cobwebs and the dust, the four men were
the only objects there which were not a
part of the structure. Strange enough they
looked in the yellow light of the candle.
The one who had so reluctantly alighted
was especially " spectacular "—he might
have been called sensational. He was of
middle age, heavily built, deep chested, and
broad shouldered. Looking at his figure,
one would have said that he had a giant's
strength ; at his face, that he would use it
like a giant. He was clean shaven, his hair
rather closely cropped and gray. His low
forehead was seamed with wrinkles above
the eyes, and over the nose these became vertical. The heavy black brows followed the same law, saved from meeting
only by an upward turn at what would
otherwise have been the point of contact.
Deeply sunken beneath these, glowed in the
obscure light a pair of eyes of uncertain
color, but, obviously enough, too small.

There was something forbidding in their
expression, which was not bettered by the
cruel mouth and wide jaw. The nose was
well enough, as noses go ; one does not
expect much of noses. All that was sinister
in the man's face seemed accentuated by an
unnatural pallor—he appeared altogether
bloodless.

The appearance of the other men was
sufficiently commonplace : they were such
persons as one meets and forgets that he
met. All were younger than the man described, between whom and the eldest of the
others, who stood apart, there was apparently no kindly feeling. They avoided looking at each other.

"Gentlemen," said the man holding the
candle and keys, "I believe everything
is right. Are you ready, Mr. Rosser?"

The man standing apart from the group
bowed and smiled.

"And you, Mr. Grossmith?"

The heavy man bowed and scowled.

"You will please remove your outer
clothing."

Their hats, coats, waistcoats, and neck-
wear were soon removed and thrown out-

side the door, in the passage. The man with the candle now nodded, and the fourth man—he who had urged Grossmith to leave the wagon—produced from the pocket of his overcoat two long, murderous-looking bowie knives which he drew from the scabbards.

"They are exactly alike," he said, presenting one to each of the two principals—for by this time the dullest observer would have understood the nature of this meeting. It was to be a duel to the death.

Each combatant took a knife, examined it critically near the candle and tested the strength of blade and handle across his lifted knee. Their persons were then searched in turn, each by the second of the other.

"If it is agreeable to you, Mr. Grossmith," said the man holding the light, "you will place yourself in that corner."

He indicated the angle of the room farthest from the door, whither Grossmith retired, his second parting from him with a grasp of the hand which had nothing of cordiality in it. In the angle nearest the door Mr. Rosser stationed himself, and, after a whispered consultation, his second left him, joining the other near the door. At that

moment the candle was suddenly extinguished, leaving all in profound darkness.
This may have been done by a draught from
the opened door ; whatever the cause, the
effect was startling.

" Gentlemen," said a voice which sounded
strangely unfamiliar in the altered condition
affecting the relations of the senses—" gentlemen, you will not move until you hear
the closing of the outer door."

A sound of trampling ensued, then the
closing of the inner door ; and finally the
outer one closed with a concussion which
shook the entire building.

A few minutes after a belated farmer's boy
met a light-wagon which was being driven
furiously toward the town of Marshall.   He
declared that behind the two figures on the
front seat stood a third, with its hands upon
the bowed shoulders of the others, who appeared to struggle vainly to free themselves
from its grasp.   This figure, unlike the
others, was clad in white, and had undoubt-
edly boarded the wagon as it passed the
haunted house.   As the lad could boast a
considerable former experience with the
supernatural thereabout, his word had the

weight justly due to the testimony of an expert. The story eventually appeared in the *Advance*, with some slight literary embellishments and a concluding intimation that the gentlemen referred to would be allowed the use of the paper's columns for their version of the night's adventure. But the privilege remained without a claimant.

II

The events which led up to this "duel in the dark" were simple enough. One evening three young men of the town of Marshall were sitting in a quiet corner of the porch of the village hotel, smoking and discussing such matters as three educated young men of a Southern village would naturally find interesting. Their names were King, Sancher, and Rosser. At a little distance, within easy hearing, but taking no part in the conversation, sat a fourth. He was a stranger to the others. They merely knew that on his arrival by the stage-coach that afternoon he had written in the hotel register the name Robert Grossmith. He had not been observed to speak to anyone except the hotel clerk. He seemed, in-

deed, singularly fond of his own company—
or, as the *personnel* of the *Advance* expressed
it, "grossly addicted to evil associations."
But then it should be said in justice to the
stranger that the *personnel* was himself of a
too convivial disposition fairly to judge one
differently gifted, and had, morever, experienced a slight rebuff in an effort at an "in-
terview."

"I hate any kind of deformity in a
woman," said King, "whether natural or
—or acquired. I have a theory that any
physical defect has its correlative mental
and moral defect."

"I infer, then," said Rosser, gravely,
"that a lady lacking the advantage of a
nose would find the struggle to become Mrs.
King an arduous enterprise."

"Of course you may put it that way,"
was the reply; "but, seriously, I once
threw over a most charming girl on learn-
ing, quite accidentally, that she had suffered amputation of a toe. My conduct was
brutal, if you like, but if I had married that
girl I should have been miserable and should
have made her so."

"Whereas," said Saucher, with a light

laugh, " by marrying a gentleman of more liberal views she escaped with a parted throat."

" Ah, you know to whom I refer ! Yes, she married Manton, but I don't know about his liberality ; I 'm not sure but he cut her throat because he discovered that she lacked that excellent thing in woman, the middle toe of the right foot."

" Look at that chap ! " said Rosser in a low voice, his eyes fixed upon the stranger.

That chap was obviously listening intently to the conversation.

" Damn his impudence ! " muttered King —" what ought we to do ? "

" That's an easy one," Rosser replied, rising. " Sir," he continued, addressing the stranger, " I think it would be better if you would remove your chair to the other end of the veranda. The presence of gentlemen is evidently an unfamiliar situation to you."

The man sprang to his feet and strode forward with clenched hands, his face white with rage. All were now standing. Sancher stepped between the belligerents.

" You are hasty and unjust," he said to

Rosser ; " this gentleman has done nothing to deserve such language."

But Rosser would not withdraw a word. By the custom of the country and the time, there could be but one outcome to the quarrel.

" I demand the satisfaction due to a gentleman," said the stranger, who had become more calm. " I have not an acquaintance in this region. Perhaps you, sir," bowing to Sancher, " will be kind enough to represent me in this matter."

Sancher accepted the trust—somewhat reluctantly, it must be confessed, for the man's appearance and manner were not at all to his liking. King, who, during the colloquy, had hardly removed his eyes from the stranger's face, and had not spoken a word, consented with a nod to act for Rosser, and the upshot of it was that, the principals having retired, a meeting was arranged for the next evening. The nature of the arrangements has been already disclosed. The duel with knives in a dark room was once a commoner feature of South-western life than it is likely to be again. How thin a veneering of " chivalry " covered the essential brutality of the code under which such encounters were possible, we shall see.

III

In the blaze of a midsummer noonday, the old Manton house was hardly true to its traditions. It was of the earth, earthy. The sunshine caressed it warmly and affectionately, with evident unconsciousness of its bad reputation. The grass greening all the expanse in its front seemed to grow, not rankly, but with a natural and joyous exuberance, and the weeds blossomed quite like plants. Full of charming lights and shadows, and populous with pleasant-voiced birds, the neglected shade trees no longer struggled to run away, but bent reverently beneath their burdens of sun and song. Even in the glassless upper windows was an expression of peace and contentment, due to the light within. Over the stony fields the visible heat danced with a lively tremor incompatible with the gravity which is an attribute of the supernatural.

Such was the aspect under which the place presented itself to Sheriff Adams and two other men who had come out from Marshall to look at it. One of these men was Mr. King, the sheriff's deputy; the other, whose name was Brewer, was a brother of the late Mrs. Manton. Under a beneficent law of the State relating to property which has been for a certain period abandoned by its owner whose residence cannot be ascertained, the sheriff was the legal custodian of the Manton farm and the appurtenances thereunto belonging. His present visit was in mere perfunctory compliance with some order of a court in which Mr. Brewer had an action to get possession of the property as heir to his deceased sister. By a mere coincidence the visit was made on the day after the night that Deputy King had unlocked the house for another and very different purpose. His presence now was not of his own choosing: he had been ordered to accompany his superior, and at the moment could think of nothing more prudent than simulated alacrity in obedience.

Carelessly opening the front door, which to his surprise was not locked, the sheriff was amazed to see, lying on the floor of the passage into which it opened, a confused heap of men's apparel. Examination showed it to consist of two hats, and the same number of coats, waistcoats, and scarfs, all in a remarkably good state of preservation, albeit somewhat defiled by the dust in which they lay. Mr. Brewer was equally astonished, but Mr. King's emotion is not of record. With a new and lively interest in his own actions, the sheriff now unlatched and pushed open a door on the right, and the three entered. The room was apparently vacant—no; as their eyes became accustomed to the dimmer light, something was visible in the farthest angle of the wall. It was a human figure—that of a man crouching close in the corner. Something in the attitude made the intruders halt when they had barely passed the threshold. The figure more and more clearly defined itself. The man was upon one knee, his back in the angle of the wall, his shoulders elevated to the level of his ears, his hands before his face, palms outward, the fingers spread and crooked like claws : the white face turned upward on the retracted neck had an expression of unutterable fright, the mouth half open, the eyes incredibly expanded.

He was stone dead. Yet, with the exception of a knife, which had evidently fallen from his own hand, not another object was in the room.

In the thick dust that covered the floor were some confused footprints near the door and along the wall through which it opened. Along one of the adjoining walls, too, past the boarded-up windows, was the trail made by the man himself in reaching his corner. Instinctively in approaching the body the three men followed that trail. The sheriff grasped one of the outthrown arms ; it was as rigid as iron, and the application of a gentle force rocked the entire body without altering the relation of its parts. Brewer, pale with excitement, gazed intently into the distorted face. "God of mercy !" he suddenly cried, "it is Manton !"

"You are right," said King, with an evident attempt at calmness : "I knew Manton. He then wore a full beard and his hair long, but this is he."

He might have added : "I recognized him when he challenged Rosser. I told Rosser and Sancher who he was before we played him this horrible trick. When Ros-

ser left this dark room at our heels, forgetting his outer clothing in the excitement,
and driving away with us in his shirt sleeves
—all through the discreditable proceedings
we knew whom we were dealing with, mur-
derer and coward that he was!"

But nothing of this did Mr. King say.
With his better light he was trying to penetrate the mystery of the man's death. That
he had not once moved from the corner
where he had been stationed, that his posture
was that of neither attack nor defense, that
he had dropped his weapon, that he had obviously perished of sheer horror of something
that he *saw*—these were circumstances which
Mr. King's disturbed intelligence could not
rightly comprehend.

Groping in intellectual darkness for a clew
to his maze of doubt, his gaze, directed mechanically downward, as is the way of one
who ponders momentous matters, fell upon
something which, there, in the light of day,
and in the presence of living companions,
struck him with an invincible terror. In
the dust of years that lay thick upon the
floor—leading from the door by which they
had entered, straight across the room to

within a yard of Manton's crouching corpse
—were three parallel lines of footprints—
light but definite impressions of bare feet,
the outer ones those of small children, the
inner a woman's. From the point at which
they ended they did not return ; they pointed
all one way. Brewer, who had observed
them at the same moment, was leaning forward in an attitude of rapt attention, horribly
pale.

"Look at that !" he cried, pointing with
both hands at the nearest print of the woman's right foot, where she had apparently
stopped and stood. "The middle toe is
missing—it was Gertrude !"

Gertrude was the late Mrs. Manton, sister
to Mr. Brewer.

A Lady from Redhorse

I FIND myself more and more interested in him. It is not, I am sure, his—do you know any good noun corresponding to the adjective "handsome?" One does not like to say "beauty" when speaking of a man. He is handsome enough, heaven knows; I should not even care to trust you with him—faithfulest of all possible wives that you are—when he looks his best, as he always does. Nor do I think the fascination of his manner has much to do with it. You recollect that the charm of art inheres in that which is undefinable, and to you and me, my dear Irene, I fancy there is rather less of that in the branch of art under considertion than to girls in their first season. I fancy I know how my fine gentleman pro-

301

duces many of his effects, and could, perhaps, give him a pointer on heightening them. Nevertheless, his manner is something truly delightful. I suppose what interests me chiefly is the man's brains. His conversation is the best I have ever heard, and altogether unlike anyone else's. He seems to know everything, as indeed he ought, for he has been everywhere, read everything, seen all there is to see—sometimes I think rather more than is good for him—and had acquaintance with the *queerest* people. And then his voice—Irene, when I hear it I actually feel as if I ought to have paid at the door, though of course it is my own door.

July 3.

I fear my remarks about Dr. Barritz must have been, being thoughtless, very silly, or you would not have written of him with such levity, not to say disrespect. Believe me, dearest, he has more dignity and seriousness (of the kind, I mean, which is not inconsistent with a manner sometimes playful and always charming) than any of the men that you and I ever met. And young Raynor— you knew Raynor at Monterey—tells me

that the men all like him, and that he is
treated with something like deference everywhere. There is a mystery, too—something
about his connection with the Blavatsky people in Northern India. Raynor either would
not or could not tell me the particulars. I
infer that Dr. Barritz is thought—don't you
dare to laugh—a magician ! Could anything
be finer than that? An ordinary mystery is
not, of course, as good as a scandal, but
when it relates to dark and dreadful prac-
tices—to the exercise of unearthly powers—
could anything be more piquant? It ex-
plains, too, the singular influence the man
has upon me. It is the undefinable in his
art—black art. Seriously, dear, I quite
tremble when he looks me full in the eyes
with those unfathomable orbs of his, which
I have already vainly attempted to describe
to you. How dreadful if he have the power
to make one fall in love ! Do you know if
the Blavatsky crowd have that power—outside of Sepoy ?

July 16.

The strangest thing ! Last evening while
Auntie was attending one of the hotel hops
(I hate them) Dr. Barritz called. It was

scandalously late—I actually believe that he had talked with Auntie in the ballroom, and learned from her that I was alone. I had been all the evening contriving how to worm out of him the truth about his connection with the Thugs in Sepoy, and all of that black business, but the moment he fixed his eyes on me (for I admitted him, I 'm ashamed to say) I was helpless, I trembled, I blushed, I—O Irene, Irene, I love the man beyond expression, and you know how it is yourself.

Fancy ! I, an ugly duckling from Red-horse—daughter (they say) of old Calamity Jim—certainly his heiress, with no living relation but an absurd old aunt, who spoils me a thousand and fifty ways—absolutely destitute of everything but a million dollars and a hope in Paris,—I daring to love a god like him ! My dear, if I had you here I could tear your hair out with mortification.

I am convinced that he is aware of my feeling, for he stayed but a few moments, said nothing but what another man might have said half as well, and pretending that he had an engagement, went away. I learned to-day (a little bird told me—the bell-bird) that he went straight to bed.

How does that strike you as evidence of exemplary habits?

JULY 17.

That little wretch, Raynor, called yesterday, and his babble set me almost wild. He never runs down—that is to say, when he exterminates a score of reputations, more or less, he does not pause between one reputation and the next. (By the way, he inquired about you, and his manifestations of interest in you had, I confess, a good deal of *vraisemblance*.) Mr. Raynor observes no game laws ; like Death (which he would inflict if slander were fatal) he has all seasons for his own. But I like him, for we knew each other at Redhorse when we were young. He was known in those days as "Giggles," and I—O Irene, can you ever forgive me?—I was called "Gunny." God knows why ; perhaps in allusion to the material of my pinafores ; perhaps because the name is in alliteration with "Giggles," for Gig and I were inseparable playmates, and the miners may have thought it a delicate compliment to recognize some kind of relationship between us.

Later, we took in a third – another of Ad-

20

versity's brood, who, like Garrick between
Tragedy and Comedy, had a chronic inability to adjudicate the rival claims of
Frost and Famine. Between him and the
grave there was seldom anything more than
a single suspender and the hope of a meal
which would at the same time support life
and make it insupportable. He literally
picked up a precarious living for himself
and an aged mother by " chloriding the
dumps," that is to say, the miners permitted
him to search the heaps of waste rock for
such pieces of " pay ore " as had been overlooked ; and these he sacked up and sold
at the Syndicate Mill. He became a mem-
ber of our firm — " Gunny, Giggles, and
Dumps " thenceforth — through my favor ;
for I could not then, nor can I now, be in-
different to his courage and prowess in de-
fending against Giggles the immemorial
right of his sex to insult a strange and unprotected female—myself. After old Jim
struck it in the Calamity, and I began to
wear shoes and go to school, and in emula-
tion Giggles took to washing his face, and
became Jack Raynor, of Wells, Fargo &
Co., and old Mrs. Barts was herself chlorided

to her fathers, Dumps drifted over to San
Juan Smith and turned stage driver, and
was killed by road agents, and so forth.

Why do I tell you all this, dear? Because
it is heavy on my heart. Because I walk
the Valley of Humility. Because I am sub-
duing myself to permanent consciousness of
my unworthiness to unloose the latchet of
Dr. Barritz's shoe. Because, oh dear, oh
dear, there 's a cousin of Dumps at this
hotel ! I have n't spoken to him. I never
had much acquaintance with him,—but do
you suppose he has recognized me? Do,
please give me in your next your candid,
sure-enough opinion about it, and say you
don't think so. Do you think He knows
about me already and that that is why He
left me last evening when He saw that I
blushed and trembled like a fool under His
eyes? You know I can't bribe *all* the newspapers, and I can't go back on anybody who
was civil to Gunny at Redhorse—not if
I 'm pitched out of society into the sea. So
the skeleton sometimes rattles behind the
door. I never cared much before, as you
know, but now—*now* it is not the same.
Jack Raynor I am sure of—he will not tell

Him. He seems, indeed, to hold Him in
such respect as hardly to dare speak to
Him at all, and I 'm a good deal that way
myself. Dear, dear ! I wish I had something besides a million dollars ! If Jack
were three inches taller I 'd marry him alive,
and go back to Redhorse and wear sack-
cloth again to the end of my miserable
days.

July 25.

We had a perfectly splendid sunset last
evening, and I must tell you all about it.
I ran away from Auntie and everybody, and
was walking alone on the beach. I expect
you to believe, you infidel ! that I had not
looked out of my window on the seaward
side of the hotel and seen Him walking alone
on the beach. If you are not lost to every
feeling of womanly delicacy you will accept
my statement without question. I soon established myself under my sunshade and
had for some time been gazing out dreamily
over the sea, when he approached, walking
close to the edge of the water—it was ebb
tide. I assure you the wet sand actually
brightened about his feet ! As he approached
me, he lifted his hat, saying, '' Miss Dement,

may I sit with you?—or will you walk with
me?"

The possibility that neither might be
agreeable seems not to have occurred to
him. Did you ever know such assurance?
Assurance? My dear, it was gall, down-
right *gall!* Well, I did n't find it worm-
wood, and replied, with my untutored
Redhorse heart in my throat, "I—I shall
be pleased to do *anything*." Could words
have been more stupid? There are depths
of fatuity in me, friend o' my soul, that are
simply bottomless!

He extended his hand, smiling, and I
delivered mine into it without a moment's
hesitation, and when his fingers closed
about it to assist me to my feet, the consciousness that it trembled made me blush
worse than the red west. I got up, however, and, after a while, observing that he
had not let go my hand, I pulled on it a
little, but unsuccessfully He simply held
on, saying nothing, but looking down
into my face with some kind of smile—I
did n't know—how could I?—whether it
was affectionate, derisive, or what, for I did
not look at him. How beautiful he was!—

with the red fires of the sunset burning in the depths of his eyes. Do you know, dear, if the Thugs and Experts of the Blavatsky region have any special kind of eyes? Ah, you should have seen his superb attitude, the godlike inclination of his head as he stood over me after I had got upon my feet! It was a noble picture, but I soon destroyed it, for I began at once to sink again to the earth. There was only one thing for him to do, and he did it ; he supported me with an arm about my waist.

" Miss Dement, are you ill ? " he said.

It was not an exclamation ; there was neither alarm nor solicitude in it. If he had added : " I suppose that is about what I am expected to say," he would hardly have expressed his sense of the situation more clearly. His manner filled me with shame and indignation, for I was suffering acutely. I wrenched my hand out of his, grasped the arm supporting me, and pushing myself free, fell plump into the sand and sat helpless. My hat had fallen off in the struggle, and my hair tumbled about my face and shoulders in the most mortifying way.

" Go away from me," I cried, half chok-

ing. "O, *please* go away, you—you Thug!
How dare you think *that* when my leg is
asleep?"

I actually said those identical words!
And then I broke down and sobbed. Irene,
I *blubbered!*

His manner altered in an instant—I could
see that much through my fingers and hair.
He dropped on one knee beside me, parted
the tangle of hair, and said, in the tender-
est way: "My poor girl, God knows I have
not intended to pain you. How should I?
—I who love you—I who have loved you
for—for years and years!"

He had pulled my wet hands away from
my face and was covering them with kisses.
My cheeks were like two coals, my whole
face was flaming, and, I think, steaming.
What could I do? I hid it on his shoulder
—there was no other place. And, O my
dear friend, how my leg tingled and thrilled,
and how I wanted to kick!

We sat so for a long time. He had released one of my hands to pass his arm about
me again, and I possessed myself of my
handkerchief and was drying my eyes and
my nose. I would not look up until that

was done ; he tried in vain to push me a little away and gaze into my face. Presently, when it was all right, and it had grown a bit dark, I lifted my head, looked him straight in the eyes, and smiled my best—my level best, dear.

" What do you mean," I said, " by ' years and years ? ' "

" Dearest," he replied, very gravely, very earnestly, " in the absence of the sunken cheeks, the hollow eyes, the lank hair, the slouching gait, the rags, dirt, and youth, can you not—will you not understand ? Gunny, I'm Dumps ! "

In a moment I was upon my feet and he upon his. I seized him by the lapels of his coat and peered into his handsome face in the deepening darkness. I was breathless with excitement.

" And you are not dead ? " I asked, hardly knowing what I said.

" Only dead in love, dear. I recovered from the road agent's bullet, but this, I fear, is fatal."

" But about Jack—Mr. Raynor ? Don't you know—"

" I am ashamed to say, darling, that it

was through that unworthy person's suggestion that I came here from Vienna."

Irene, they have roped in your affectionate
friend,

MARY JANE DEMENT.

P.S.—The worst of it is that there is no
mystery.   That was an invention of Jack to
arouse my curiosity and interest.   James
is not a Thug.   He solemnly assures me
that in all his wanderings he has never set
foot in Sepoy.

Haïta the Shepherd

IN the heart of Haïta the illusions of
youth had not been supplanted by
those of age and experience. His thoughts
were pure and pleasant, for his life was simple and his soul devoid of ambition. He
rose with the sun, and went forth to pray at
the shrine of Hastur, the god of shepherds,
who heard and was pleased. After performance of this pious rite Haïta unbarred the
gate of the fold, and with a cheerful mind
drove his flock afield, eating his morning
meal of curds and oat cake as he went, occasionally pausing to add a few berries, cold
with dew, or to drink of the waters that
came away from the hills to join the stream
in the middle of the valley and be borne
along with it, he knew not whither.

During the long summer day, as his sheep
cropped the good grass which the gods had

made to grow for them, or lay with their fore-legs doubled under their breasts and indolently chewed the cud, Haïta, reclining in the shadow of a tree, or sitting upon a rock, played so sweet music upon his reed pipe that sometimes from the corner of his eye he got accidental glimpses of the minor sylvan deities, leaning forward out of the copse to hear ; but if he looked at them directly, they vanished.   From this—for he must be thinking if he would not turn into one of his own sheep—he drew the solemn inference that happiness may come if not sought, but if looked for will never be seen ; for, next to the favor of Hastur, who never disclosed himself, Haïta most valued the friendly interest of his neighbors, the shy immortals of the wood and stream.   At nightfall he drove his flock back to the fold, saw that the gate was secure, and retired to his cave for refreshment and for dreams.

So passed his life, one day like another, save when the storms uttered the wrath of an offended god.   Then Haïta cowered in his cave, his face hidden in his hands, and prayed that he alone might be punished for his sins and the world saved from destruction. Sometimes when there was a great rain, and the stream came out of its banks, compelling him to urge his terrified flock to the uplands, he interceded for the people in the cities which he had been told lay in the plain beyond the two blue hills forming the gateway of his valley.

"It is kind of thee, O Hastur," so he prayed, "to give me mountains so near to my dwelling and my fold that I and my sheep can escape the angry torrents; but the rest of the world thou must thyself deliver in some way that I know not of, or I will no longer worship thee."

And Hastur, knowing that Haïta was a youth who kept his word, spared the cities and turned the waters into the sea.

So he had lived since he could remember. He could not rightly conceive any other mode of existence. The holy hermit who dwelt at the head of the valley, a full hour's journey away, from whom he had heard the tale of the great cities where dwelt people— poor souls !—who had no sheep, gave him no knowledge of that early time, when, so he reasoned, he must have been small and helpless like a lamb.

It was through thinking on these myster-
ies and marvels, and on that horrible change
to silence and decay which he felt sure must
sometime come to him, as he had seen it
come to so many of his flock—as it came to
all living things except the birds—that Haïta
first became conscious how miserable was
his lot.

"It is necessary," he said, "that I know
whence and how I came ; for how can one
perform his duties unless able to judge what
they are by the way in which he was intrusted with them ? And what contentment
can I have when I know not how long it is
going to last ? Perhaps before another sun
I may be changed, and then what will become of the sheep? What, indeed, will have
become of me ? "

Pondering these things, Haïta became
melancholy and morose. He no longer spoke
cheerfully to his flock, nor ran with alacrity
to the shrine of Hastur. In every breeze he
heard whispers of malign deities whose existence he now first observed. Every cloud
was a portent signifying disaster, and the
darkness was full of new terrors. His reed
pipe when applied to his lips gave out no

melody but a dismal wail ; the sylvan and
riparian intelligences no longer thronged
the thicket-side to listen, but fled from the
sound, as he knew by the stirred leaves and
bent flowers. He relaxed his vigilance, and
many of his sheep strayed away into the
hills and were lost. Those that remained became lean and ill for lack of good pasturage,
for he would not seek it for them, but con-
ducted them day after day to the same spot,
through mere abstraction, while puzzling
about life and death—of immortality he
knew not.

One day, while indulging in the gloomiest
reflections, he suddenly sprang from the rock
upon which he sat, and, with a determined
gesture of the right hand, exclaimed : " I
will no longer be a suppliant for knowledge
which the gods withhold. Let them look to
it that they do me no wrong. I will do my
duty as best I can, and if I err, upon their
own heads be it."

Suddenly, as he spoke, a great brightness
fell about him, causing him to look upward,
thinking the sun had burst through a rift in
the clouds ; but there were no clouds.
No more than an arm's length away stood

a beautiful maiden. So beautiful she was that the flowers about her feet folded their petals in despair and bent their heads in token of submission ; so sweet her look that the humming birds thronged her eyes, thrusting their thirsty bills almost into them, and the wild bees were about her lips. And such was her brightness that the shadows of all objects lay divergent from her feet, turning as she moved.

Haïta was entranced. Rising, he knelt before her in adoration, and she laid her hand upon his head.

"Come," she said in a voice which had the music of all the bells of his flock—"come, thou art not to worship me, who am no goddess, but if thou art truthful and dutiful, I will abide with thee."

Haïta seized her hand, and stammering his joy and gratitude arose, and hand in hand they stood and smiled in each other's eyes. He gazed upon her with reverence and rapture. He said : "I pray thee, lovely maid, tell me thy name and whence and why thou comest."

At this she laid a warning finger on her lip and began to withdraw. Her beauty underwent a visible alteration that made him shudder, he knew not why, for still she was beautiful. The landscape was darkened by a giant shadow sweeping across the valley with the speed of a vulture. In the obscurity the maiden's figure grew dim and indistinct and her voice seemed to come from a distance, as she said, in a tone of sorrowful reproach : " Presumptuous and ungrateful youth ! must I then so soon leave thee? Would nothing do but thou must at once break the eternal compact ? "

Inexpressibly grieved, Haïta fell upon his knees and implored her to remain—rose and sought her in the deepening darkness—ran in circles, calling to her aloud, but all in vain. She was no longer visible, but out of the gloom he heard her voice saying : " Nay, thou shalt not have me by seeking. Go to thy duty, faithless shepherd, or we never meet again."

Night had fallen, the wolves were howling in the hills, and the terrified sheep crowding about his feet. In the demands of the hour he forgot his disappointment, drove his flock to the fold, and repairing to the place of worship poured out his heart in gratitude to Hastur for permitting him to save his flock, then retired to his cave and slept.

When Haïta awoke, the sun was high and shone in at his cave, illuminating it with a great glory. And there, beside him, sat the maiden. She smiled upon him with a smile that seemed the visible music of his pipe of reeds. He dared not speak, fearing to offend her as before, for he knew not what he could venture to say.

"Because," she said, "thou didst thy duty by the flock, and didst not forget to thank Hastur for staying the wolves of the night, I am come to thee again. Wilt thou have me for a companion?"

"Who would not have thee forever?" replied Haïta. "Oh! never again leave me until—until I—change and become silent and motionless."

Haïta had no word for death.

"I wish, indeed," he continued, "that thou wert of my own sex, that we might wrestle and run races and so never tire of being together."

At these words the maiden arose and passed out of the cave, and Haïta, springing

from his couch of fragrant boughs to over-
take and detain her, observed, to his astonishment, that the rain was falling and the
stream in the middle of the valley had come
out of its banks. The sheep were bleating
in terror, for the rising waters had invaded
their fold. And there was danger for the
unknown cities of the distant plain.

It was many days before Haïta saw the
maiden again. One day he was returning
from the head of the valley, where he had
gone with ewe's milk and oat cake and berries for the holy hermit, who was too old
and feeble to provide himself with food.

"Poor old man!" he said aloud, as he
trudged along homeward. "I will return
to-morrow and bear him on my back to my
own dwelling, where I can care for him.
Doubtless it is for that that Hastur has
reared me all these years, and gives me
health and strength."

As he spoke, the maiden, clad in glittering
garments, met him in the path with a smile
which took away his breath.

"I am come again," she said, "to dwell
with thee if thou wilt now have me, for none
else will. Thou mayest have learned wisdom,

and art willing to take me as I am, nor care
to know."

Haïta threw himself at her feet. "Beautiful being," he cried, "if thou wilt but deign
to accept all the devotion of my heart and
soul—after Hastur be served—it is yours forever. But, alas! thou art capricious and
wayward. Before to-morrow's sun I may
lose thee again. Promise, I beseech thee, that
however in my ignorance I may offend, thou
wilt forgive and remain always with me."

Scarcely had he finished speaking when a
troops of bears came out of the hills, racing
toward him with crimson mouths and fiery
eyes. The maiden again vanished, and he
turned and fled for his life. Nor did he stop
until he was in the cot of the holy hermit,
whence he had set out. Hastily barring
the door against the bears, he cast himself
upon the ground and wept.

"My son," said the hermit from his
couch of straw, freshly gathered that morning
by Haïta's hands, "it is not like thee to weep
for bears—tell me what sorrow has befallen
thee, that age may minister to the hurts of
youth with such balms as it hath of its
wisdom."

Haïta told him all : how thrice he had met the radiant maid, and thrice she had left him forlorn. He related minutely all that had passed between them, omitting no word of what had been said.

When he had ended, the holy hermit was a moment silent, then said : " My son, I have attended to thy story, and I know the maiden. I have myself seen her, as have many. Know, then, that her name, which she would not even permit thee to inquire, is Happiness. Thou saidst the truth to her, that she was capricious, for she imposeth conditions that man cannot fulfill, and delinquency is punished by desertion. She cometh only when unsought, and will not be questioned. One manifestation of curiosity, one sign of doubt, one expression of misgiving, and she is away ! How long didst thou have her at any time before she fled ? "

" But a single instant," answered Haïta, blushing with shame at the confession. " Each time I drove her away in one moment."

" Unfortunate youth !" said the holy hermit, " but for thine indiscretion thou mightst have had her for two."

The Damned Thing

I

ONE DOES NOT ALWAYS EAT WHAT IS ON THE TABLE

BY the light of a tallow candle, which had been placed on one end of a rough table, a man was reading something written in a book. It was an old account book, greatly worn; and the writing was not, apparently, very legible, for the man sometimes held the page close to the flame of the candle to get a stronger light upon it. The shadow of the book would then throw into obscurity a half of the room, darkening a number of faces and figures; for besides the reader, eight other men were present. Seven of them sat against the rough log walls, silent and motionless, and, the room being

small, not very far from the table. By extending an arm any one of them could have
touched the eighth man, who lay on the table, face upward, partly covered by a sheet,
his arms at his sides. He was dead.

The man with the book was not reading
aloud, and no one spoke ; all seemed to be
waiting for something to occur ; the dead
man only was without expectation. From
the blank darkness outside came in, through
the aperture that served for a window, all
the ever unfamiliar noises of night in the
wilderness—the long nameless note of a distant coyote ; the stilly pulsing thrill of tireless insects in trees ; strange cries of night
birds, so different from those of the birds of
day ; the drone of great blundering beetles,
and all that mysterious chorus of small
sounds that seem always to have been but
half heard when they have suddenly ceased,
as if conscious of an indiscretion. But nothing of all this was noted in that company ;
its members were not overmuch addicted to
idle interest in matters of no practical importance ; that was obvious in every line of their
rugged faces—obvious even in the dim light
of the single candle. They were evidently

men of the vicinity—farmers and woodmen.

The person reading was a trifle different; one would have said of him that he was of the world, worldly, albeit there was that in his attire which attested a certain fellowship with the organisms of his environment. His coat would hardly have passed muster in San Francisco: his foot-gear was not of urban origin, and the hat that lay by him on the floor (he was the only one uncovered) was such that if one had considered it as an article of mere personal adornment he would have missed its meaning. In countenance the man was rather prepossessing, with just a hint of sternness; though that he may have assumed or cultivated, as appropriate to one in authority. For he was a coroner. It was by virtue of his office that he had possession of the book in which he was reading; it had been found among the dead man's effects—in his cabin, where the inquest was now taking place.

When the coroner had finished reading he put the book into his breast pocket. At that moment the door was pushed open and a young man entered. He, clearly, was not of mountain birth and breeding: he was

clad as those who dwell in cities. His clothing was dusty, however, as from travel. He
had, in fact, been riding hard to attend the
inquest.

The coroner nodded ; no one else greeted
him.

"We have waited for you," said the coroner. "It is necessary to have done with
this business to-night."

The young man smiled. "I am sorry to
have kept you," he said. "I went away,
not to evade your summons, but to post to
my newspaper an account of what I suppose I am called back to relate."

The coroner smiled.

"The account that you posted to your
newspaper," he said, "differs, probably from
that which you will give here under oath."

"That," replied the other, rather hotly
and with a visible flush, "is as you choose.
I used manifold paper and have a copy of
what I sent. It was not written as news,
for it is incredible, but as fiction. It may
go as a part of my testimony under oath."

"But you say it is incredible."

"That is nothing to you, sir, if I also
swear that it is true."

The coroner was apparently not greatly affected by the young man's manifest resentment. He was silent for some moments, his eyes upon the floor. The men about the sides of the cabin talked in whispers, but seldom withdrew their gaze from the face of the corpse. Presently the coroner lifted his eyes and said : "We will resume the inquest."

The men removed their hats. The witness was sworn.

"What is your name?" the coroner asked.

"William Harker."

"Age?"

"Twenty-seven."

"You knew the deceased, Hugh Morgan?"

"Yes."

"You were with him when he died?"

"Near him."

"How did that happen—your presence, I mean?"

"I was visiting him at this place to shoot and fish. A part of my purpose, however, was to study him, and his odd, solitary way of life. He seemed a good model for a character in fiction. I sometimes write stories.''

'' I sometimes read them.''

'' Thank you.''

'' Stories in general—not yours.''

Some of the jurors laughed. Against a sombre background humor shows high lights. Soldiers in the intervals of battle laugh easily, and a jest in the death chamber conquers by surprise.

'' Relate the circumstances of this man's death,'' said the coroner. '' You may use any notes or memoranda that you please.''

The witness understood. Pulling a manuscript from his breast pocket he held it near the candle, and turning the leaves until he found the passage that he wanted began to read.

II

WHAT MAY HAPPEN IN A FIELD OF WILD OATS

'' . . . THE sun had hardly risen when we left the house. We were looking for quail, each with a shotgun, but we had only one dog. Morgan said that our best ground was beyond a certain ridge that he pointed out, and we crossed it by a trail through the *chapparal*. On the other side was comparatively level ground, thickly covered with wild oats. As we emerged from the *chapparal*, Morgan was but a few yards in advance. Suddenly, we heard, at a little distance to our right, and partly in front, a noise as of some animal thrashing about in the bushes, which we could see were violently agitated.

"'We've started a deer,' I said. 'I wish we had brought a rifle.'

"Morgan, who had stopped and was intently watching the agitated *chapparal*, said nothing, but had cocked both barrels of his gun, and was holding it in readiness to aim. I thought him a trifle excited, which surprised me, for he had a reputation for exceptional coolness, even in moments of sudden and imminent peril.

"'O, come!' I said. 'You are not going to fill up a deer with quail-shot, are you?'

"Still he did not reply ; but, catching a sight of his face as he turned it slightly toward me, I was struck by the pallor of it.

Then I understood that we had serious business on hand, and my first conjecture was
that we had 'jumped' a grizzly. I advanced
to Morgan's side, cocking my piece as I
moved.

"The bushes were now quiet, and the
sounds had ceased, but Morgan was as attentive to the place as before.

"'What is it? What the devil is it?' I
asked.

"'That Damned Thing!' he replied,
without turning his head. His voice was
husky and unnatural. He trembled visibly.

"I was about to speak further, when I
observed the wild oats near the place of the
disturbance moving in the most inexplicable
way. I can hardly describe it. It seemed
as if stirred by a streak of wind, which not
only bent it, but pressed it down—crushed
it so that it did not rise, and this movement
was slowly prolonging itself directly toward
us.

"Nothing that I had ever seen had affected
me so strangely as this unfamiliar and unac-
countable phenomenon, yet I am unable to
recall any sense of fear. I remember—and

tell it here because, singularly enough, I recollected it then—that once, in looking carelessly out of an open window, I momentarily mistook a small tree close at hand for one of a group of larger trees at a little distance away. It looked the same size as the others, but, being more distinctly and sharply defined in mass and detail, seemed out of harmony with them. It was a mere falsification of the law of aerial perspective, but it startled, almost terrified me. We so rely upon the orderly operation of familiar natural laws that any seeming suspension of them is noted as a menace to our safety, a warning of unthinkable calamity. So now the apparently causeless movement of the herbage, and the slow, undeviating approach of the line of disturbance were distinctly disquieting. My companion appeared actually frightened, and I could hardly credit my senses when I saw him suddenly throw his gun to his shoulder and fire both barrels at the agitated grass ! Before the smoke of the discharge had cleared away I heard a loud savage cry—a scream like that of a wild animal—and, flinging his gun upon the ground, Morgan sprang away and ran swiftly from the spot, At the same instant I was thrown violently to the ground by the impact of something unseen in the smoke—some soft, heavy substance that seemed thrown against me with great force.

"Before I could get upon my feet and recover my gun, which seemed to have been struck from my hands, I heard Morgan crying out as if in mortal agony, and mingling with his cries were such hoarse savage sounds as one hears from fighting dogs. Inexpressibly terrified, I struggled to my feet and looked in the direction of Morgan's retreat ; and may Heaven in mercy spare me from another sight like that ! At a distance of less than thirty yards was my friend, down upon one knee, his head thrown back at a frightful angle, hatless, his long hair in disorder and his whole body in violent movement from side to side, backward and forward. His right arm was lifted and seemed to lack the hand—at least, I could see none. The other arm was invisible. At times, as my memory now reports this extraordinary scene, I could discern but a part of his body ; it was as if he had been partly blotted out— I cannot otherwise express it—then a shifting of his position would bring it all into view again.

"All this must have occurred within a few seconds, yet in that time Morgan assumed all the postures of a determined wrestler vanquished by superior weight and strength. I saw nothing but him, and him not always distinctly. During the entire incident his shouts and curses were heard, as if through an enveloping uproar of such sounds of rage and fury as I had never heard from the throat of man or brute !

"For a moment only I stood irresolute, then, throwing down my gun, I ran forward to my friend's assistance. I had a vague belief that he was suffering from a fit, or some form of convulsion. Before I could reach his side he was down and quiet. All sounds had ceased, but, with a feeling of such terror as even these awful events had not inspired, I now saw the same mysterious movements of the wild oats prolonging itself from the trampled area about the prostrate man towards the edge of a wood. It was only when it had reached the wood that I was able to withdraw my eyes and look at my companion. He was dead."

III

A MAN THOUGH NAKED MAY BE IN RAGS

THE coroner rose from his seat and stood beside the dead man. Lifting an edge of the sheet he pulled it away, exposing the entire body, altogether naked and showing in the candle light a claylike yellow. It had, however, broad maculations of bluish black, obviously caused by extravasated blood from contusions. The chest and sides looked as if they had been beaten with a bludgeon. There were dreadful lacerations; the skin was torn in strips and shreds.

The coroner moved round to the end of the table and undid a silk handkerchief, which had been passed under the chin and knotted on the top of the head. When the handkerchief was drawn away it exposed what had been the throat. Some of the jurors who had risen to get a better view repented their curiosity, and turned away their faces. Witness Harker went to the open window and leaned out across the sill, faint and sick. Dropping the handkerchief upon the dead man's neck the coroner stepped to an angle of the room, and from a pile of clothing produced one garment after another, each of which he held up a moment for inspection. All were torn, and stiff with blood. The jurors did not make a closer inspection. They seemed rather uninterested. They had, in truth, seen all this before; the only thing that was new to them being Harker's testimony.

"Gentlemen," the coroner said, "we have no more evidence, I think. Your duty has been already explained to you; if there is nothing you wish to ask you may go outside and consider your verdict."

The foreman rose—a tall, bearded man of sixty, coarsely clad.

"I should like to ask one question, Mr. Coroner," he said. "What asylum did this yer last witness escape from?"

"Mr. Harker," said the coroner, gravely and tranquilly, "from what asylum did you last escape?"

Harker flushed crimson again, but said nothing, and the seven jurors rose and solemnly filed out of the cabin.

"If you have done insulting me, sir," said Harker, as soon as he and the officer were left alone with the dead man, " I suppose I am at liberty to go?"

"Yes."

Harker started to leave, put paused, with his hand on the door latch. The habit of his profession was strong in him—stronger than his sense of personal dignity. He turned about and said :

"The book that you have there—I recognize it as Morgan's diary. You seemed greatly interested in it ; you read in it while I was testifying. May I see it? The public would like—"

" The book will cut no figure in this matter," replied the official, slipping it into his coat pocket ; all the entries in it were made before the writer's death."

As Harker passed out of the house the jury re-entered and stood about the table, on which the now covered corpse showed under the sheet with sharp definition. The foreman seated himself near the candle, produced from his breast pocket a pencil and scrap of paper, and wrote rather laboriously, the following verdict, which with various degrees of effort all signed :

" We, the jury, do find that the remains

come to their death at the hands of a mountain lion, but some of us thinks, all the same, they had fits."

IV

AN EXPLANATION FROM THE TOMB

IN the diary of the late Hugh Morgan are certain interesting entries having, possibly, a scientific value as suggestions. At the inquest upon his body the book was not put in evidence ; possibly the coroner thought it not worth while to confuse the jury. The date of the first of the entries mentioned cannot be ascertained ; the upper part of the leaf is torn away ; the part of the entry remaining is as follows :

" . . . would run in a half circle, keeping his head turned always toward the centre, and again he would stand still, barking furiously. At last he ran away into the brush as fast as he could go. I thought at first that he had gone mad, but on returning to the house found no other alteration in his manner than what was obviously due to fear of punishment.

" Can a dog see with his nose ? Do odors

impress some olfactory centre with images
of the thing emitting them?　.　.　.

"Sept. 2.—Looking at the stars last nigh
as they rose above the crest of the ridge east
of the house, I observed them successively
disappear—from left to right. Each was
eclipsed but an instant, and only a few at
the same time, but along the entire length
of the ridge all that were within a degree or
two of the crest were blotted out. It was
as if something had passed along between
me and them ; but I could not see it, and
the stars were not thick enough to define its
outline. Ugh ! I don't like this. . . ."

Several weeks' entries are missing, three
leaves being torn from the book.

" Sept. 27.—It has been about here again
—I find evidences of its presence every day.
I watched again all of last night in the same
cover, gun in hand, double-charged with
buckshot. In the morning the fresh footprints were there, as before. Yet I would
have sworn that I did not sleep—indeed, I
hardly sleep at all. It is terrible, insupportable ! If these amazing experiences are real
I shall go mad ; if they are fanciful I am
mad already.

"Oct. 3.—I shall not go—it shall not drive me away. No, this is *my* house, *my* land. God hates a coward. . . .

"Oct. 5.—I can stand it no longer; I have invited Harker to pass a few weeks with me —he has a level head. I can judge from his manner if he thinks me mad.

"Oct 7.—I have the solution of the problem; it came to me last night—suddenly, as by revelation. How simple—how terribly simple!

"There are sounds that we cannot hear. At either end of the scale are notes that stir no cord of that imperfect instrument, the human ear. They are too high or too grave. I have observed a flock of blackbirds occupying an entire tree-top—the tops of several trees—and all in full song. Suddenly—in a moment—at absolutely the same instant— all spring into the air and fly away. How? They could not all see one another—whole tree-tops intervened. At no point could a leader have been visible to all. There must have been a signal of warning or command, high and shrill above the din, but by me unheard. I have observed, too, the same simultaneous flight when all were silent, among not only blackbirds, but other birds—quail, for example, widely separated by bushes— even on opposite sides of a hill.

" It is known to seamen that a school of whales basking or sporting on the surface of the ocean, miles apart, with the convexity of the earth between them, will sometimes dive at the same instant—all gone out of sight in a moment. The signal has been sounded—too grave for the ear of the sailor at the masthead and his comrades on the deck—who nevertheless feel its vibrations in the ship as the stones of a cathedral are stirred by the bass of the organ.

" As with sounds, so with colors. At each end of the solar spectrum the chemist can detect the presence of what are known as ' actinic ' rays. They represent colors— integral colors in the composition of light— which we are unable to discern. The human eye is an imperfect instrument ; its range is but a few octaves of the real ' chromatic scale.' I am not mad ; there are colors that we cannot see.

" And, God help me ! the Damned Thing is of such a color ! "

The Eyes of the Panther

I

ONE DOES NOT ALWAYS MARRY WHEN IN-SANE

A MAN and a woman—nature had done
the grouping—sat on a rustic seat, in
the late afternoon. The man was middle-
aged, slender, swarthy, with the expression
of a poet and the complexion of a pirate—a
man at whom one would look again. The
woman was young, blonde, graceful, with
something in her figure and movements suggesting the word "lithe." She was habited
in a gray gown with odd brown markings
in the texture. She may have been beautiful; one could not readily say, for her eyes
denied attention to all else. They were gray-
green, long and narrow, with an expression
defying analysis. One could only know

that they were disquieting. Cleopatra may have had such eyes.

The man and the woman talked.

"Yes," said the woman, "I love you, God knows! But marry you, no. I cannot, will not."

"Irene, you have said that many times, yet always have denied me a reason. I've a right to know, to understand, to feel and prove my fortitude if I have it. Give me a reason."

"For loving you?"

The woman was smiling through her tears and her pallor. That did not stir any sense of humor in the man.

"No; there is no reason for that. A reason for not marrying me. I've a right to know. I must know. I will know!"

He had risen and was standing before her with clenched hands, on his face a frown—it might have been called a scowl. He looked as if he might attempt to learn by strangling her. She smiled no more—merely sat looking up into his face with a fixed, set regard that was utterly without emotion or sentiment. Yet it had something in it that tamed his resentment and made him shiver.

"You are determined to have my reason?" she asked in a tone that was entirely mechanical—a tone that might have been her look made audible.

"If you please—if I'm not asking too much."

Apparently this lord of creation was yielding some part of his dominion over his co-creature.

"Very well, you shall know: I am insane."

The man started, then looked incredulous and was conscious that he ought to be amused. But again the sense of humor failed him in his need, and despite his disbelief he was profoundly disturbed by that which he did not believe. Between our convictions and our feelings there is no good understanding.

"That is what the physicians would say," the woman continued — "if they knew. I might myself prefer to call it a case of 'possession.' Sit down and hear what I have to say."

The man silently resumed his seat beside her on the rustic bench by the wayside. Over against them on the eastern side of the valley the hills were already sunset-flushed and the stillness all about was of that peculiar quality which foretells the twilight. Something of its mysterious and significant solemnity had imparted itself to the man's mood. In the spiritual, as in the material world, are signs and presages of night. Rarely meeting her look, and whenever he did so conscious of the indefinable dread with which, despite their feline beauty, her eyes always affected him, Jenner Brading listened in silence to the story told by Irene Marlowe. In deference to the reader's possible prejudice against the artless method of an unpracticed historian the author ventures to substitute his own version for hers.

II

A ROOM MAY BE TOO NARROW FOR THREE, THOUGH ONE IS OUTSIDE

In a little log-house containing a single room sparely and rudely furnished, crouching on the floor against one of the walls, was a woman, clasping to her breast a child. Outside, a dense unbroken forest extended

for many miles in every direction. This
was at night and the room was black dark :
no human eye could have discerned the woman and the child. Yet they were observed,
narrowly, vigilantly, with never a momen-
tary slackening of attention ; and that is the
pivotal fact upon which this narrative turns.

Charles Marlowe was of the class, now extinct in this country, of woodmen pioneers—
men who found their most acceptable surroundings in sylvan solitudes that stretched
along the eastern slope of the Mississippi
Valley, from the great lakes to the Gulf of
Mexico. For more than two hundred years
these men pushed ever westward, generation after generation, with rifle and ax, re-
claiming from Nature and her savage
children here and there an isolated acreage
for the plow, no sooner reclaimed than
surrendered to their less venturesome but
more thrifty successors. At last they burst
through the edge of the forest into the open
country and vanished as if they had fallen
over a cliff. The woodman pioneer is no
more ; the pioneer of the plains—he whose
easy task it was to subdue for occupancy two-
thirds of the country in a single genera-

tion—is another and inferior creation. With
Charles Marlowe in the wilderness, sharing
the dangers, hardships and privations of
that strange, unprofitable life, were his wife
and child, to whom, in the manner of his
class, in which the domestic virtues were a
religion, he was passionately attached. The
woman was still young enough to be comely,
new enough to the awful isolation of her lot
to be cheerful. By withholding the large
capacity for happiness which the simple satis-
factions of the forest life could not have
filled, Heaven had dealt honorably with her.
In her light household tasks, her child, her
husband and her few foolish books, she
found abundant provision for her needs.

One morning in midsummer Marlowe took
down his rifle from the wooden hooks on
the wall and signified his intention of getting game.

"We've meat enough," said the wife;
"please don't go out to-day. I dreamed
last night, O, such a dreadful thing! I
cannot recollect it, but I'm almost sure that
it will come to pass if you go out."

It is painful to confess that Marlowe received this solemn statement with less of

gravity than was due to the mysterious nature of the calamity foreshadowed. In truth,
he laughed.

"Try to remember," he said. "Maybe
you dreamed that Baby had lost the power
of speech."

The conjecture was obviously suggested
by the fact that Baby, clinging to the fringe
of his hunting-coat with all her ten pudgy
thumbs was at that moment uttering her
sense of the situation in a series of exultant
goo-goos inspired by sight of her father's
raccoon-skin cap.

The woman yielded : lacking the gift of
humor she could not hold out against his
kindly badinage. So, with a kiss for the
mother and a kiss for the child, he left the
house and closed the door upon his happiness forever.

At nightfall he had not returned. The
woman prepared supper and waited. Then
she put Baby to bed and sang softly to her
until she slept. By this time the fire on the
hearth, at which she had cooked supper,
had burned out and the room was lighted
by a single candle. This she afterward
placed in the open window as a sign and

welcome to the hunter if he should approach from that side. She had thoughtfully closed and barred the door against such wild animals as might prefer it to an open window—of the habits of beasts of prey in entering a house uninvited she was not advised, though with true female prevision she may have considered the possibility of their entrance by way of the chimney. As the night wore on she became not less anxious, but more drowsy, and at last rested her arms upon the bed by the child and her head upon the arms. The candle in the window burned down to the socket, sputtered and flared a moment and went out unobserved; for the woman slept. And sleeping she dreamed.

In her dreams she sat beside the cradle of a second child. The first one was dead. The father was dead. The home in the forest was lost and the dwelling in which she lived was unfamiliar. There were heavy oaken doors, always closed, and outside the windows, fastened into the thick stone walls, were iron bars, obviously (so she thought) a provision against Indians. All this she noted with an infinite self-pity, but without surprise—an emotion unknown in dreams.

The child in the cradle was invisible under its coverlet which something impelled her to remove. She did so, disclosing the face of a wild animal ! In the shock of this dreadfull revelation the dreamer awoke, trembling in the darkness of her cabin in the wood.

As a sense of her actual surroundings came slowly back to her she felt for the child that was not a dream, and assured herself by its breathing that all was well with it ; nor could she forbear to pass a hand lightly across its face. Then, moved by some impulse for which she probably could not have accounted, she rose and took the sleeping babe in her arms, holding it close against her breast. The head of the child's cot was against the wall to which the woman now turned her back as she stood. Lifting her eyes she saw two bright objects starring the darkness with a reddish-green glow. She took them to be two coals on the hearth, but with her returning sense of direction came the disquieting consciousness that they were not in that quarter of the room, moreover were too high, being nearly at the level of her eyes—of her own eyes. For these were the eyes of a panther.

The beast was at the open window directly opposite and not five paces away. Nothing but those terrible eyes were visible, but in the dreadful tumult of her feelings as the situation disclosed itself to her understanding she somehow knew that the animal was standing on its hinder feet, supporting itself with its paws on the window-ledge. That signified a malign interest—not the mere gratification of an indolent curiosity. The consciousness of the attitude was an added horror, accentuating the menace of those awful eyes, in whose steadfast fire her strength and courage were alike consumed. Under their silent questioning she shuddered and turned sick. Her knees failed her, and by degrees, instinctively striving to avoid a sudden movement that might bring the beast upon her, she sank to the floor, crouched against the wall and tried to shield the babe with her trembling body without withdrawing her gaze from the luminous orbs that were killing her. No thought of her husband came to her in her agony—no hope nor suggestion of rescue or escape. Her capacity for thought and feeling had narrowed to the dimensions of a single emotion—fear of the

animal's spring, of the impact of its body,
the buffeting of its great arms, the feel of its
teeth in her throat, the mangling of her
babe. Motionless now and in absolute silence, she awaited her doom, the moments
growing to hours, to years, to ages ; and
still those devilish eyes maintained their
watch.

Returning to his cabin late at night with
a deer on his shoulder Charles Marlowe tried
the door. It did not yield. He knocked ;
there was no answer. He laid down his
deer and went round to the window. As he
turned the angle of the building he fancied
he heard a sound as of stealthy footfalls and
a rustling in the undergrowth of the forest,
but they were too slight for certainty, even to
his practised ear. Approaching the window,
and to his surprise finding it open, he threw
his leg over the sill and entered. All was
darkness and silence. He groped his way
to the fire-place, struck a match and lit
a candle. Then he looked about. Cow-
ering on the floor against a wall was his wife,
clasping his child. As he sprang toward
her she broke into laughter, long, loud, and
mechanical, devoid of gladness and devoid

of sense—the laughter that is not out of
keeping with the clanking of a chain.
Hardly knowing what he did he extended
his arms. She laid the babe in them. It
was dead—pressed to death in its mother's
embrace.

III

THE THEORY OF THE DEFENSE

THAT is what occurred during a night in
a forest, but not all of it did Irene Marlowe
relate to Jenner Brading ; not all of it was
known to her. When she had concluded
the sun was below the horizon and the long
summer twilight had begun to deepen in the
hollows of the land. For some moments
Brading was silent, expecting the narrative
to be carried forward to some definite connection with the conversation introducing
it ; but the narrator was as silent as he, her
face averted, her hands clasping and unclasp-
ing themselves as they lay in her lap, with
a singular suggestion of an activity indepen-
dent of her will.

"It is a sad, a terrible story," said Brading at last, "but I do not understand. You

call Charles Marlowe father ; that I know. That he is old before his time, broken by some great sorrow, I have seen, or thought I saw. But, pardon me, you said that you —that you—''

'' That I am insane,'' said the girl, without a movement of head or body.

'' But, Irene, you say—please, dear, do not look away from me—you say that the child was dead, not demented.''

'' Yes, that one—I am the second. I was born three months after that night, my mother being mercifully permitted to lay down her life in giving me mine.''

Brading was again silent ; he was a trifle dazed and could not at once think of the right thing to say. Her face was still turned away. In his embarrassment he reached impulsively toward the hands that lay closing and unclosing in her lap, but something—he could not have said what-- restrained him. He then remembered, vaguely, that he had never altogether cared to take her hand.

'' Is it likely,'' she resumed, '' that a person born under such circumstances is like others—is what you call sane ? ''

Brading did not reply ; he was preoccupied with a new thought that was taking shape in his mind—what a scientist would have called an hypothesis, a detective a theory. It might throw an added light, albeit a lurid one, upon such doubt of her sanity as her own assertion had not dispelled.

The country was still new and, outside the villages, sparsely populated. The professional hunter was still a familiar figure, and among his trophies were heads and pelts of the larger kinds of game. Tales variously credible of nocturnal meetings with savage animals in lonely roads were sometimes current, passed through the customary stages of growth and decay, and were forgotten. A recent addition to these popular apocrypha, originating, apparently, by spontaneous generation in several households, was of a panther which had frightened some of their members by looking in at windows by night. The yarn had caused its little ripple of excitement—had even attained to the distinction of a place in the local newspaper ; but Brading had given it no attention. Its likeness to the story to

which he had just listened now impressed
him as perhaps more than accidental. Was
it not possible that the one story had suggested the other—that finding congenial
conditions in a morbid mind and a fertile
fancy, it had grown to the tragic tale that
he had heard?

Brading recalled certain circumstances of
the girl's history and disposition, of which,
with love's incuriosity, he had hitherto
been heedless—such as her solitary life with
her father, at whose house no one, apparently, was an acceptable visitor and her
strange fear of the night, by which those
who knew her best accounted for her never
being seen after dark. Surely in such a
mind imagination once kindled might burn
with a lawless flame, penetrating and enveloping the entire structure. That she was
mad, though the conviction gave him the
acutest pain, he could no longer doubt ; she
had only mistaken an effect of her mental
disorder for its cause, bringing into imaginary relation with her own personality the
vagaries of the local myth-makers. With
some vague intention of testing his new
"theory," and no very definite notion of

how to set about it, he said, gravely, but with hesitation :

"Irene, dear, tell me—I beg you will not take offence, but tell me——"

"I have told you," she interrupted, speaking with a passionate earnestness that he had not known her to show—"I have already told you that we cannot marry ; is anything else worth saying ? "

Before he could stop her she had sprung from her seat, and without another word or look was gliding away among the trees toward her father's house. Brading had risen to detain her ; he stood watching her in silence until she had vanished in the gloom. Suddenly he started as if he had been shot ; his face took on an expression of amazement and alarm ; in one of the black shadows into which she had disappeared he had caught a quick brief glimpse of shining eyes. For an instant he was dazed and irresolute ; and then, he dashed into the wood after her, shouting : "Irene, Irene, look out ! The panther ! The panther ! "

In a moment he had passed through the fringe of forest into open ground and saw the girl's gray skirt vanishing into her father's door. No panther was visible.

IV

AN APPEAL TO THE CONSCIENCE OF GOD

JENNER BRADING, attorney-at-law, lived in a cottage at the edge of the town. Directly behind the dwelling was the forest. Being a bachelor, and therefore, by the Draconian moral code of the time and place denied the services of the only species of domestic servant known thereabout, the "hired girl," he boarded at the village hotel, where also was his office. The woodside cottage was merely a lodging maintained—at no great cost, to be sure—as an evidence of prosperity and respectability. It would hardly do for one to whom the local newspaper had pointed with pride as "the foremost jurist of his time" to be "homeless," albeit he may sometimes have suspected that the words "home" and "house" were not strictly synonymous. Indeed, his consciousness of the disparity and his will to harmonize it were matters of logical inference, for it was generally believed that soon after the cottage was built its owner had made a futile venture in the direction of marriage—had, in truth, gone so far as to be rejected by the beautiful but eccentric daughter of Old Man Marlowe, the recluse. This was publicly believed because he had told it himself and she had not—a reversal of the usual order of things which could hardly fail to carry conviction.

Brading's bedroom was at the rear of the house, with a single window facing the forest. One night he was awakened by a noise at that window; he could hardly have said what it was like. With a little thrill of the nerves he sat up in bed and laid hold of the revolver which, with a forethought most commendable in one addicted to the habit of sleeping on the ground floor with an open window, he had put under his pillow. The room was in absolute darkness, but being unterrified he knew where to direct his eyes, and there he held them, awaiting in silence what further might occur. He could now dimly discern the aperture—a square of lighter black. Suddenly there appeared at its lower edge two

gleaming eyes that burned with a malignant lustre inexpressibly horrible ! Brading's heart gave a great jump then seemed
to stand still. A chill passed along his
spine and through his hair ; he felt the
blood forsake his cheeks. He could not
have cried out—not to save his life ; but
being a man of courage he would not, to
save his life, have done so if he had been
able. Some trepidation his coward body
might feel, but his spirit was of sterner stuff.
Slowly the shining eyes rose with a steady
motion that seemed an approach, and slowly
rose Brading's right hand, holding the pistol. He fired !

Blinded by the flash and stunned by
the report, Brading nevertheless heard, or
fancied that he heard, the wild, high scream
of the panther, so human in sound, so
devilish in suggestion. Leaping from the
bed he hastily clothed himself and pistol
in hand, sprang from the door, meeting two
or three men who came running up from
the road. A brief explanation was followed
by a cautious search at the rear of the house.
The grass was wet with dew ; beneath the
window it had been trodden and partly lev-

elled for a wide space, from which a devious trail, visible in the light of a lantern, led away into the bushes. One of the men stumbled and fell upon his hands, which, as he rose and rubbed them together, were slippery. On examination they were seen to be red with blood.

An encounter, unarmed, with a wounded panther was not agreeable to their taste; all but Brading turned back. He, with lantern and pistol, pushed courageously forward into the wood. Passing through a difficult undergrowth he came into a small opening, and there his courage had its reward, for there he found the body of his victim. But it was no panther. What it was is told, even to this day, upon a weather-worn headstone in the village churchyard, and for many years was attested daily at the graveside by the bent figure and sorrow-seamed face of Old Man Marlowe, to whose soul, and to the soul of his strange, unhappy child, peace. Peace and reparation.

THE END

THE HUDSON LIBRARY.

Registered as second-class matter.

16°, paper, 50 cts. ; 12°, cloth, $1.00 and $1.25.

1. **Love and Shawl-Straps.**   By ANNETTE LUCILE NOBLE.

2. **Miss Hurd: An Enigma.**   By ANNA KATHARINE GREEN.

3. **How Thankful was Bewitched.**   By J. K. HOSMER.

4. **A Woman of Impulse.**   By JUSTIN HUNTLEY McCARTHY.

5. **Countess Bettina.**   By CLINTON ROSS.

6. **Her Majesty.**   By ELIZABETH K. TOMPKINS.

7. **God Forsaken.**   By FREDERIC BRETON.

8. **An Island Princess.**   By THEODORE GIFT.

9. **Elizabeth's Pretenders.**   By HAMILTON AÏDÉ.

10. **At Tuxter's.**   By G. B. BURGIN.

11. **At Cherryfield Hall.**   By FREDERIC H. BALFOUR.

12. **The Crime of the Century.**   By R. OTTOLENGUI.

13. **The Things that Matter.**   By FRANCIS GRIBBLE.

14. **The Heart of Life.**   By W. H. MALLOCK.

G. P. PUTNAM'S SONS, NEW YORK & LONDON.

THE HUDSON LIBRARY.

G. P. PUTNAM'S SONS, New York & London.

THE UNIVERSITY SERIES

I. Harvard Stories. Sketches of the Undergraduate. By W. K. POST. Fifteenth edition. 12°, paper, 50 cts.; cloth, $1.00.

" Not since the days of *Hammersmith* have we had such a vivid picture of college life as Mr. W. K. Post has given us in this book. Unpretentious, in their style, the stories are mere sketches, yet withal the tone is so genuine, the local color so truly ' crimson,' as to make the book one of unfailing interest."—*Literary World.*

II. Yale Yarns. By J. S. WOOD. Fifth edition. Illustrated, 12°, $1.00.

" A bright, realistic picture of college life, told in an easy conversational, or descriptive style, and cannot fail to genuinely interest the reader who has the slightest appreciation of humor. The volume is illustrated and is just the book for an idle or a lonely hour."—*Los Angeles Times.*

III. The Babe, B.A. Stories of Life at Cambridge University. By EDW. F. BENSON. Illustrated, 12°, $1.00.

" The story tells of the every-day life of a young man called the Babe. . . . Cleverly written and one of the best this author has written."—*Leader*, New Haven.

IV. A Princetonian. A Story of Undergraduate Life at the College of New Jersey. By JAMES BARNES. Illustrated, 12°, $1.25.

" It is fresh, hearty, sensible, and readable, leaving a good impression of college life upon the mind."—*Baltimore Sun.*

BY ANNA KATHARINE GREEN

The Leavenworth Case. A Lawyer's Story. 4°, paper, 20 cts.; 16°, paper, 50 cts.; cloth, $1.00.

" She has worked up a *cause célèbre* with a fertility of device and ingenuity of treatment hardly second to Wilkie Collins or Edgar Allan Poe."—*Christian Union.*

" . . . Told with a force and power that indicate great dramatic talent in the writer."—*St. Louis Post.*

Hand and Ring. Popular edition. 4°, paper, 20 cts.; 16°, paper, illustrated, 50 cts.; cloth, $1.00.

" The best, most intricate, most perfectly constructed, and most fascinating detective story ever written."—*Utica Herald.*

Marked "Personal." 16°, paper, 50 cts.; cloth, $1.00.

" It is a tribute to the author's genius that she never tires and never loses her readers. It moves on, clean and healthy, and ends without raising images or making impressions which have to be forgotten."—*Boston Journal.*

That Affair Next Door. Hudson Library, No. 17. Seventh edition. 12°, paper, 50 cts.; cloth, $1.00.

Other works by Anna Katharine Green are as follows: " A Strange Disappearance," " The Sword of Damocles," " The Mill Mystery," " Behind Closed Doors," " X. Y. Z.," " 7 to 12," " The Old Stone House," " Cynthia Wakeham's Money," " The Doctor, His Wife, and the Clock," " Dr. Izard."

G. P. PUTNAM'S SONS, NEW YORK AND LONDON.